The Sewing Bee
By The Sea

De-ann Black

Toffee
Apple

Toffee Apple Publishing

Other books in the Cottages, Cakes & Crafts book series are:

Book 1 - The Flower Hunter's Cottage.
Book 2 - The Sewing Bee by the Sea.
Book 3 - The Beemaster's Cottage.
Book 4 - The Chocolatier's Cottage
Book 5 - The Bookshop by the Seaside

Text copyright © 2015 by De-ann Black
Cover Design & Illustration © 2015 by De-ann Black

All rights reserved.
No part of this book may be used or reproduced in any manner
whatsoever without the written consent of the publisher.

This is a work of fiction. Names, characters, places, and incidents
are either products of the author's imagination or are used
fictitiously. Any resemblance to actual persons, living or dead,
businesses, companies, events, or locales is entirely coincidental.

Published by Toffee Apple Publishing 2015

The Sewing Bee by the Sea

ISBN: 9781520781464

Toffee
Apple

Toffee Apple Publishing

Also by De-ann Black (Romance, Action/Thrillers & Children's books). See her Amazon Author page or website for further details about her books, screenplays, illustrations, art and fabric designs.
www.De-annBlack.com

Romance:

The Sewing Shop
Heather Park
The Tea Shop by the Sea
The Bookshop by the Seaside
The Sewing Bee
The Quilting Bee
Snow Bells Wedding
Snow Bells Christmas
Summer Sewing Bee
The Chocolatier's Cottage
Christmas Cake Chateau
The Beemaster's Cottage
The Sewing Bee By The Sea
The Flower Hunter's Cottage

The Christmas Knitting Bee
The Sewing Bee & Afternoon Tea
The Vintage Sewing & Knitting Bee
Shed In The City
The Bakery By The Seaside
Champagne Chic Lemonade Money
The Christmas Chocolatier
The Christmas Tea Shop & Bakery
The Vintage Tea Dress Shop In Summer
Oops! I'm The Paparazzi
The Bitch-Proof Suit

Action/Thrillers:

Love Him Forever.
Someone Worse.
Electric Shadows.

The Strife Of Riley.
Shadows Of Murder.

Children's books:

Faeriefied.
Secondhand Spooks.
Poison-Wynd.

Wormhole Wynd.
Science Fashion.
School For Aliens.

Colouring books:

Summer Garden. Spring Garden. Autumn Garden. Sea Dream.
Festive Christmas. Christmas Garden. Flower Bee. Wild Garden.
Faerie Garden Spring. Flower Hunter. Stargazer Space. Bee Garden.

Embroidery books:

Floral Nature Embroidery Designs
Scottish Garden Embroidery Designs

Contents

CHAPTER ONE

The Dressmaker

I received a mysterious letter with an equally mysterious message from someone who signed their name as — *the dressmaker.*

The letter arrived early on a windswept day in May. Outside the window of my flat, the city looked grey. A bleak morning, in more ways than one. The first Saturday I hadn't gone to work in two years.

I worked in a department store in the city centre. I'd recently been passed over for promotion. I wasn't totally surprised. I was realistic enough to know there was little chance my sales assistant position would be upped to lower management in the soft furnishings department. They advised me to apply again in another two years. I'd be thirty by then. And earlier in the week a memo had gone round informing staff that redundancies were in the offing. My hours were cut.

I'd tried to cheer myself up with the thought of enjoying a Saturday off, relaxing at home with my feet up, eating a lingering breakfast and not having to deal with the city traffic and yet another day selling cushions, curtains and knick–knackery. But it was difficult to be cheery when my job prospects were as bleak as the watery grey sky.

If the letter had arrived a few weeks earlier, I wouldn't have re–read it, taking its offer seriously.

Dear Tiree, I'd like you to come and have afternoon tea with me at my cottage. A map is enclosed showing the location in the Highlands. It's less than a two hour drive away. I hope you'll decide to come and chat. I should've retired years ago, but I'm still making dresses that earn me a considerable amount of money, and I'm looking for a new apprentice. I'd like to teach my skills to you, and want to discuss offering you a two–year dressmaking apprenticeship with me. All the details will be discussed when you arrive. You would have a rented cottage to live in and earn more money than you make working at the department store.

1

I'm offering you a better future. If you think it's worth the drive up to meet me, bring an overnight bag. You may wish to spend the weekend here.

If it's any further incentive — I knew your mother. I taught her dressmaking when you were a little girl. So I know you too.

I look forward to seeing you.

The dressmaker.

A smattering of rain hit off the window. I remembered some of the things my mother told me about learning to sew beautiful evening gowns from a dressmaker who lived in a cottage. I wished I could remember more, but I was barely four years old when we left the Highlands, and I had no real recollection of living there — just flashes of summer days, the seashore, flower gardens and feeling happy, despite everything, including having no father. He'd left my mother before I was born and we'd never been in contact. He'd treated her poorly and I never wanted to know him. She said he was the reason we left our home up north and went to live in the city where there was more work for her. While I was growing up, she worked as a seamstress. We were never affluent and often had to scrimp and save, but we were happy in our own way, always sewing and crafting things — making do and mending.

I made most of my own clothes and home furnishings. My world was an eclectic mix of pretty curtains in the kitchen and rich velvet drapes in the living room, with everything brightened by colourful rag rugs and novelty cushion covers appliquéd with seahorse motifs, fairy cakes and flowers. I loved to sew and I loved the sea, even though I lived in the city. Perhaps somewhere deep inside I did remember where I was born, in a seaside location in the Highlands. We always said that one day we'd go back. We never did.

When I lost her two years ago, I lost our home in the city too as the lease was in her name and they didn't want to continue it with me. I had to find a flat. Life had, to say the least, become darker.

We'd worked together from home sewing dresses and home accessories and selling them online. We didn't make a lot of profit, but it paid the rent and kept us solvent, and we enjoyed working together. We had our sewing machines, cutting table and basically a little work shop set up in the living room. This was something else I lost along with the house.

The first month on my own in the flat was difficult. The thought of setting up the sewing and craft business again seemed daunting. It was too much for me at the time. I opted for a job at the department store instead — a hard route to take to make life seem easier.

I gazed out at the weary day and reckoned I had two choices. I could sit here sipping a cup of tea and flick through the television channels, or throw some things in an overnight bag and drive north. I'd already showered and tidied my hair, forgetting I didn't have to go to work, so all I needed was to grab a bag and head out on a small adventure. Something I hadn't done in a long, long time.

I drove out of the city and took the main route to the Highlands. I had the dressmaker's map with me to keep me right.

In an hour and a half I was at the beautiful little harbour, a key location. I was to stop at the post office and ask directions from there. So I did.

The postmaster looked at me with such curiosity I felt compelled to explain I'd received a letter from the dressmaker.

'The dressmaker has invited me to have afternoon tea with her, but I've never been to her cottage and have no idea where it is.'

'It's tricky to find. Far up in the forest.' He saw a man go by the front window. 'Hang on a minute.' He ran after the man. I watched the postmaster talk animatedly to a tall, rather handsome man whose hair was as dark as his warm jacket. He wore the collar up against the wind which emphasised the manly contours of his face. The man frowned and then glanced in the window at me, as if I was indeed a curiosity.

The postmaster beckoned me to come outside and introduced me to the man.

'This is Tavion. He's a flower grower. He knows how to get to the dressmaker's cottage.'

'My car is parked over there.' Tavion pointed across the road. Waves washed up along the harbour walls. The sea was as grey as the sky. Along the stretch of coast a band of thunderous pink clouds amid the grey warned of an approaching storm heading inland. A scattering of white cottages had a view of the sea. A row of little shops added pops of colour to the beautiful rugged landscape. One cottage stood on its own. It was the palest pink with a garden with two cherry trees covered in pink blossom that had the potential to outdo the others. I liked it. It had a stillness to it, as if no one lived there.

Tavion's voice broke into my thoughts. 'I'll lead the way. It's not far, just twisty–turny.'

I brushed my long, fair hair away from my eyes. The wind whipped it in all directions.

'Thanks,' I said to both the postmaster and Tavion.

The postmaster hurried back inside the post office out of the biting wind, while I drove after Tavion. We drove along part of the coast that led to a countryside road, and then the road narrowed and became dense with trees. Tavion's sturdy four–by–four vehicle handled the road better than my car but I kept up. It didn't take long to arrive outside the dressmaker's cottage that had as mysterious an air to it as the letter.

Trees arched around the traditional, two–storey cottage and all sorts of greenery clambered up the walls and across the lintels. The scent of the trees and grass filtered through the air.

Tavion got out of his car and came over to me. 'Here's my phone number. Call me when you want to find your way back. I live nearby.'

'Thanks for your trouble.'

He smiled and waved as he left. 'No trouble at all.'

The curtains in the front window of what appeared to be the living room twitched, twice. I'd been spotted.

The front door opened and a woman in her late fifties nodded to me and smiled. She had a friendly face and a flurry of salt and pepper curls. She was small and robust, wearing a skirt, blouse and cardigan.

'Come away in, Tiree. The dressmaker is delighted you're here.'

I blinked at the sound of my name. No one had called me by my full name in years. No one except my mother. Everyone called me Ree. I'd given up having people ask me whether I came from Tiree in Scotland, which I didn't, and had cut it short to Ree. Even the management at work addressed me as Ree.

I was escorted into the most unexpected living room. Filled with shelves of gorgeous fabric, floor to ceiling, neat and tidy, everything polished to perfection. A very beautiful woman of retirement age sat at a table near the patio doors. The doors led on to a lovely garden.

The whole place could've been used as a film set for a vintage drama and not needed a stitch altered.

And yet...it didn't feel old–fashioned. It felt just right, as if it had hit the perfect note in the past and had stayed that way, pitch perfect for decades. No modern equivalent I'd ever seen could improve on it.

Pale blue–grey painted walls peeped from behind the shelves, and the rich and vibrant colours of the silks, satins, chambrays and herringbone fabrics gave an extraordinary fairytale quality to the cottage.

'Thank you for coming here.' The dressmaker reached out her hand.

Her fingers were delicate, like the rest of her, but when we shook hands I felt a tremendous strength, strength of character, of will, from one seemingly so fragile.

'It's lovely to see you again. You've become a beautiful young woman.' Her lips wavered. There was a lie in there. I knew how tired I looked these days. Worn and weary. The harshness of life had taken the edge off any sense of prettiness I'd ever felt.

'Sit down and we'll chat while we have our tea.' She smiled up at the woman. 'This is Judith. She's my assistant and a dear friend.'

Judith nodded and went away to make the tea. The table was already set with floral china.

'You said you knew my mother.' I couldn't wait to ask, eager for any details.

'Yes, she was one of my apprentices years ago. Before you were born and shortly afterwards.'

'I'm sorry, I don't remember you.' I wished I could. I searched her pale features that blended with her cream dress and cardigan. She would've been a blonde, like me, in her youth, though silver was now her dominant shade. She wore her hair in an elegant bun, and a modicum of makeup.

'You were only three or four at the time. I remember you playing in the garden, running through the long grass and the flowers in a little blue and lemon summer dress your mother made for you. You complained that the dress was too long, and we took the hem up for you.'

I remembered that day. I had a photograph taken by my mother. I was wearing the dress and standing in the garden. I couldn't

5

remember any details. I glanced out the patio doors. Obviously it had been the dressmaker's garden. We'd lived in rented accommodation attached to a farmhouse and it was more rough grass than cultivated flowers and a lawn.

The dressmaker clasped her hands and leaned forward earnestly. 'I promised your mother I'd look out for you.' Frown lines broke across her forehead. 'I know I should have contacted you sooner. However, when I heard about what happened with your mother I wanted to give you time to find yourself, to settle. Then I heard you'd started dating a young man, a manager at the department store, and I didn't want to interfere.'

It should've felt odd that she'd been keeping tabs on my life and yet I didn't feel uncomfortable. There was nothing threatening in her manner and I knew how often I'd wanted to reach out to my past but instead had let the years drift on. How easy it was to think of doing something but never actually doing it.

Judith poured our tea into china cups and then went back through to the kitchen.

'How did you know where to find me?' I asked the dressmaker.

Light blue eyes looked directly at me. 'You crossed my mind recently. You weren't difficult to find. There are few with your surname and even fewer called Tiree. Judith searched the web and found out you still lived and worked in the city. We found your address and I sent the letter, hoping you'd come and join us.'

Judith came through with a tray of cakes decorated with fondant tea roses and a plate of dainty sandwiches. She put them down on the table which was covered with a lilac linen tablecloth embroidered at the edges with flowers. 'Help yourself to the cakes and sandwiches, Tiree.'

'Call me, Ree. That's what everyone calls me.' Except my mother. She'd never shortened it. I smiled at Judith, thinking she'd take what I said without question.

Judith glanced at the dressmaker who didn't mince her words even though her tone was soft. 'Do you know how long your mother took to decide a name for you? A name she was sure you'd love?'

I shook my head.

'All the time she was expecting you. *Should I call my little girl Tiree? Should I call her Skye? No, Tiree is such a beautiful name. She's bound to love it.* And we all agreed.'

6

'I do love it. But people always ask about it. It's easier to just be Ree.'

'Well,' the dressmaker said, leaning back in her chair, 'while you're here, you'll be you again. Not Ree.'

Her slight rebuke should've stung, but it didn't.

She stirred her tea. 'Regarding your dressmaking skills...I've also been waiting until you'd gained enough experience, developed your own style of sewing.'

'I don't sew these days. I haven't stitched anything for two years.'

Judith looked aghast, as if I'd said something hideous. 'You gave up sewing?'

'Yes.'

'Why?' said Judith.

'No time, no inclination, no purpose.' No one to share it with.

The phone rang. Judith answered it. 'Yes, yes she is. One moment.' She cupped her hand over the mouthpiece. 'It's Los Angeles,' she whispered, giving the dressmaker a knowing look.

The dressmaker got up to take the call. 'I'm sorry, Tiree. I have to take this. It's very important business.'

I nodded and wondered where to go to give her privacy. Judith ushered me through to the kitchen with her.

She sat me down at the kitchen table and poured me a cup of tea. The kitchen was a match for the living room in decor and classic styling. We sat opposite each other.

I thought her spectacles were going to steam up as she said to me, 'You gave up *sewing*? We saw some of the dresses and other items you and your mother made and sold online. They were beautiful.'

I explained about not feeling up to it, living alone in the flat and everything I'd lost.

Judith pressed her lips firmly together and nodded her understanding. I sensed no more would be made of this matter.

'The dressmaker won't take long with the phone call. It's a stylist in Hollywood asking about dresses they need sewn for a special event for their clients. We've had a lot of interest shown in our new dresses. When I say our dresses, I really mean the dressmaker's designs. I'm not a seamstress. I help out with everything else, leaving her time to concentrate on her sewing and pattern making.'

'Does the dressmaker have a name?'

'Yes, but we don't use it. It doesn't suit her. She's the dressmaker. That's what she does, what she is, and that's what we call her.'

'Fair enough.' I sipped my tea.

Judith's movements were quick, unlike the dressmaker who had a languid quality to her. 'The dressmaker rarely asks to see anyone these days.' She spoke in a confiding tone. 'And there's something you should know, whether you believe or understand.'

'Understand what?'

'The dressmaker has the gift. She's what you would call...fey.'

I took a moment to think about this. 'So she can see into the future?'

Judith adjusted her spectacles. 'Not exactly, but sort of.'

I looked at her.

'I know that sounds a bit confusing, but sometimes things aren't easily explained. She often knows things about people, things you couldn't really know unless you were fey.' She sat her cup down. 'She doesn't know everything. Not at all, but she gets feelings about things and she's usually right, so listen to what she tells you. You'll learn to sew a lot better and —'

'I haven't said I'll take the offer,' I was quick to mention.

Judith gave me a look.

'Okay,' I relented, 'so you think I'll come and work here.'

She nodded.

'The letter mentioned a cottage.'

'A lovely cottage down by the sea. Think carefully about turning down an offer like that.'

I gazed down into my cup and thought about all the things I'd have to do to leave the city and move here. It was daunting.

'I remember you as well,' said Judith, jolting me.

'Do you?'

She nodded emphatically. 'You were a nice wee girl. Loved playing in the garden while your mother and the dressmaker sewed in the house. We had a picnic on the lawn one day. You liked to pour juice and lemonade into our cups from your dolly's teapot. You were a right wee girly girl.'

I felt upset.

Judith leaned across and squeezed my hand. 'Don't upset yourself. I know you don't remember. You were too young. I'm just trying to reassure you. You're not alone in the world. We remember you. You could build a new life here for yourself. The dressmaker encourages her apprentices to be independent. She doesn't want a clone of herself. She's had a hard winter. Her hands aren't as rock steady as they used to be, not after a fierce winter, but once she's had some sunlight and warmer weather, she'll be fine. However, she's had orders for four special dresses, each one worth a wee fortune. All for Hollywood. She's promised to sew each dress and have them ready within eight weeks. She's designed the patterns. I emailed them. That's what the phone call is about. They've got to approve of the dress designs. Then she'll start cutting and sewing. The only problem is the cutting.' She looked right at me. 'And that's where you come in. You'll have to cut the patterns.'

The dressmaker called to Judith, cutting short our conversation. We went back through to have our afternoon tea.

'I was just explaining to Tiree about the pattern cutting for the dresses,' said Judith.

The dressmaker smiled at me. 'Judith is brilliant at everything — except the cutting.'

Judith put one of the sandwiches on her side plate. 'I get nervous when it comes to cutting beautiful fabric, especially if it's taken weeks to embroider or embellish it.' She made her hands tremble. 'I worry I'll faff it up.' She laughed. 'And of course, because I'm shaky about it, I always bloomin' faff it up.'

I laughed lightly and helped myself to a tomato and cheese sandwich and one of the fondant rose cakes.

'So we're locking the door,' Judith joked, 'and not letting you go until you've cut the pattern pieces.'

Any tension in the atmosphere lifted and we continued having our tea and chatting about the details of the apprenticeship.

It took another pot of tea, all the sandwiches and half the cakes to get round to the nitty–gritty details of the cottage accommodation.

'I've taken on the lease of a local cottage for a year. It will probably be available continually. It's down at the harbour. Perhaps you noticed it. The pink cottage near the post office.'

'Yes, pale pink. Very pretty.'

9

'It's not actually pink. It's warm white, but the light from the sea makes it look pink, depending on the weather. You'll stay there. You'll come up here to learn from me, then practise in your own cottage.'

Sewing in a cottage by the sea? My heart soared.

'The woman who lived there has retired and gone to stay with relatives in America,' the dressmaker explained. 'She used to work from home, as many of the people do around here. She made jam, and her kitchen has an extension set up for the jam making. It's been cleared now that the cottage is leased, and I thought it would be ideal for setting up your sewing machine. Plenty of space to create your own sewing room, and you can step out into the back garden. You'll have space and privacy.'

I sensed both aspects were important to the dressmaker.

'They used to call it the strawberry jam cottage. Probably still will, even though you'll be sewing instead of making jam.'

'I like the name,' I told her.

The dressmaker glanced out the window. 'I'd like you to see the cottage in the daylight.' It was late afternoon and the grey clouds had brought with them an early twilight. 'Judith, could you show Tiree the cottage?'

Five minutes later I drove down the twisty forest road towards the harbour with Judith giving me directions from the passenger seat.

I tried to memorise the route. Overshadowed by trees, the scenery hadn't quite warmed up to the idea that this was May and summer was in the offing. Of all the seasons in Scotland, I'd always found the transition from spring to summer the least predictable. April showers could be followed by sunshine so bright it made the city streets sparkle. May should be mild, but blustery winds and thunder storms weren't unusual. The previous summer in the city it had rained throughout June, but a heatwave in August made up the deficit in sunny days. Here, it seemed more likely to be unpredictable due to the merging of the sea with the miles of countryside that rose up to the bank of forest where the dressmaker's cottage was situated. Fluctuations in the weather didn't bother me. I was just happy to breath in the fresh air.

Carpets of bluebells created a misty quality around the base of the trees. Two trees covered in white blossom stood out from the dark greenery. This was where the road curved tightly like the tail of a seahorse, and as we emerged from the forest the sea came into view.

We arrived outside the pink cottage. Judith had the keys and showed me around.

'It's furnished but not overwhelming. There's plenty of room for your things, especially through here.' Judith led me through to the kitchen which had a large extension with two, long wooden tables, chairs and shelving.

'It smells faintly of strawberry jam.'

'The aroma will fade once you're living here and have the kitchen door and windows open.'

'I don't mind. It smells delicious.'

'Her jam was tasty.' Judith opened the cupboard doors and cabinets. 'Everything's been thoroughly cleaned and ready for someone moving in. I hope it'll be you.'

I was already nodding. The thought of having to go back to the confines of a dank flat made me shudder.

Judith smiled at me. 'Great. The silversmith will help us get your belongings transported here from the city.'

'A silversmith?'

'He dabbles in various trades, including house clearances and removals. We've spoken to him about the possibility of you coming here and he's happy to provide manpower and transport. And I'll go with you to help with the packing.'

'I don't have a lot of belongings. I'd like to bring my sewing machines, the things that belonged to my mother, and all my sewing stuff and personal items. The rest...well...

'Anything you don't want, he'll dispose of it for you. Think of it as a fresh start.'

I was.

She showed me round the two bedrooms with their wardrobes, beds and chests of drawers. 'We've got plenty of linen you can use. And there will be lots of handy extras from the welcoming party.'

I frowned.

'Oh yes, you'll need to have a party and invite people over for a wee house warming. It's the done thing. Again, I'll help you, and I know Ethel will too. She remembers you as well.'

'Ethel?' The name struck deep into my thoughts.

'Do you remember her?'

'I'm not sure.'

'Ethel used to baby sit you when I was busy helping the dressmaker and your mother. She's about the same age as the dressmaker. They went to school together in Falkirk.'

'So the dressmaker isn't originally from here?'

'She is, but her parents were busy and had no time for her. They sent her to live with her aunt in Falkirk. Her aunty was a seamstress and taught her to sew. She lived there until she was in her teens. Then they passed away and she inherited the cottage in the forest. Ethel came to live in one of the cottages here — the blue cottage. They've been friends for years, though nowadays the dressmaker keeps herself to herself.'

'What does Ethel look like?' Then I corrected myself. 'What did she look like?'

'Beautiful. Blonde. Always smiling and laughing. An expert at knitting. She still is. She runs her yarn business from her cottage.'

'The blonde lady. I've had pictures of her in my mind for years. Someone who reminded me of sunny days. Laughing, smiling.'

'Ethel will be delighted to see you again.'

She finished showing me around the cottage. I stepped out into the back garden. The cherry trees were covered in pink blossom. There was a small lawn and flower beds bursting with daffodils, tulips and a blue flower I didn't recognise.

'That's viper's bugloss. Fantastic blue colour. The dressmaker has them in her garden.'

'I'm not really a gardener, but I'll make an effort to keep this lovely.'

'The flower hunter planted most of it. He lives in the cottage with the most beautiful garden you'll ever see. A heritage garden, filled with plants from all over the world.'

'It sounds wonderful. He's certainly made the most of this little garden.' Flowers blossomed around the edges of the path in vibrant yellows and lilacs.

'Tavion often adds new bulbs when needed. It's amazing what men will do in exchange for a jar of homemade strawberry jam,' she added lightly.

'I suppose I'll have to plant my own flowers until they can be bribed with sewing.'

'Oh I think a young woman with your looks and character will have no problem attracting the attention of some of our eligible men. There are quite a few round here. Tavion's single, and the silversmith is a heartbreaker so don't say you haven't been warned.'

'There must be something in the air that breeds gorgeous men round here.'

'Fresh air, a relaxed but hard working lifestyle.' Judith shrugged. 'The dressmaker thinks it's also to do with forces that draw people to where they are meant to be.'

'Like me?'

'Yes, but you'll still have to watch you don't end up smitten and have your heart broken. Love carefully.'

'Is that even feasible?'

She shrugged again. 'I was married for over twenty–five years. I still miss him. But I have the dressmaker, my friends like Ethel, Thimble and now you to look out for.'

'Who's Thimble?'

'He's the dressmaker's cat. Thimble the fifth if we're being picky.'

'I love cats.'

'You'll love Thimble. He'll be home for his dinner soon.' She checked the time. 'And so should we. Come on, you can tell the dressmaker you're coming to work with us. I'll make something extra delicious for our dinner.'

I insisted that she didn't prompt me so I could navigate the way back to the dressmaker's cottage. I almost got it in one. I'd get it totally right next time.

'Tiree's moving here,' Judith announced as soon as we walked into the living room.

The smile the dressmaker gave me warmed my heart. 'That's wonderful. We're going to have an exciting, challenging and extraordinary time. We'll make dresses the world will see and admire.'

There was an uplifting atmosphere and lots of giggling as the three of us set about making dinner, chatting about our plans and wondering if I should attempt to cut some of the dress patterns after dinner.

Filled with enthusiasm I said, 'Yes, definitely. I'll cut the patterns out tonight and we'll make a start on sewing the dresses.' Hollywood, here we go.

CHAPTER TWO

Strawberry Jam Cottage

I hadn't sewn in two years, but I'd sewn all my life. After dinner the dressmaker and Judith showed me the sewing room. I'd been so mesmerised by the shelves packed with fabric in the living room, I hadn't noticed the door leading through to what was once a bedroom, now transformed into the sewing room of my dreams. If I hadn't seen the cottage by the sea, I could've been persuaded to move in here.

It was lit by daylight lamps with shades that deflected any glare, like creating perpetual and perfect daylight conditions for sewing and seeing the colours of the fabrics.

There were several sewing machines. Some of them were the latest models I longed to own but couldn't have afforded — from vintage treadle machines and a long arm quilter, to overlockers and computerised sewing machines that altered stitch types, tension and lengths at the push of a button. It had a walk–in haberdashery cupboard with threads and notions galore — ribbon, trims, bias binding, sequins, lace and silk lining. There was a wall of chiffon, organza, tulle and other sheer fabrics that looked like a fairytale frieze, each roll of fabric creating a haze of colour against the white backdrop. Jewel tones of velvet were piled on the shelves and a glass jar labelled *threaded gold embellishments* shone with eighteen carat brilliance.

Dressmaking scissors and other accoutrements hung in order of size on top of a French dresser. One peek inside the dresser drawers made me gasp. I'd never seen so many types of beads — from seed pearls and bugle beads to crystals of every hue you could need to match a fabric.

The room was a treasure in itself. It was practical and magnificent in equal measures.

I gazed around and murmured, 'It has everything we need to sew the dresses.'

'To create magic,' the dressmaker said, smiling. It wasn't the first time she'd hinted that a little magic was sewn into the dresses.

'Magic of the heart, for the love of sewing,' she gave as an explanation.

I nodded, still taking everything in. I'd never seen anything like this. I felt myself smile just looking at it.

The dressmaker sat down at her sewing table and flicked on a computer screen to the left of the table. A pattern layout appeared in view and various options for fabrics were displayed down the side. 'We have to be both sensible and sensational.'

'Difficult,' I said.

The dressmaker acknowledged this was true. 'However, the sensibility comes from our clever use of fabric to create an atmosphere, a feeling. A dress is just a dress, even if it's made from beautiful fabric, if it doesn't evoke a sense, a feeling of an era or a season. And that's where we begin.'

She gestured to me to sit beside her.

Judith handed me a copy of the brief. I skimmed the list of requirements. Two leading actresses needed two dresses. Each of the four dresses had to be different from the others, and yet equally stunning. The dresses would be worn to movie premiere events — one event in Hollywood, the opening premiere, followed by one in London. The weather had to be taken into consideration.

'Luckily it'll still be summery in London,' said Judith, and then she left us and went to make a pot of tea.

'Rain is always a possibility,' the dressmaker said. 'And we may make that work to our advantage.'

She seemed to have a clear idea of what she wanted. Where did I fit in?

'Shall we get started, Tiree?'

'Yes,' I replied.

The dressmaker took a deep breath. 'You're sort of being thrown into this, but I know you have the ability. The dresses you used to sew had aspects we're going to use. So, let me ask you first. When you think about four different dresses, as described in the brief, what do you picture? What comes first? The cut, the colour, the fabric?'

I hesitated.

'It's not a test, Tiree. I do want to teach you some of the skills I know, but I need you to stretch your abilities now, quickly, to help me make these dresses. What do you think of? What do you see?'

'The colours,' I said. 'I picture strong classics — black, red, gold, silver. If it was only one dress, perhaps I'd think of the fabric. Red chiffon, black velvet, shimmering gold organza and sparkling silver lamé.'

The dressmaker looked thoughtful. 'That would usually be sufficient, and I'm sure the dresses you'd make would look lovely, but how would you like to take a step into a different league?'

I nodded eagerly.

'Don't think in terms of what colour the dresses should be,' she said. 'Don't think of the fabric, not yet. Think instead of creating a feeling, an atmosphere, as I already mentioned.'

'I'm not sure how to do that,' I told her.

'Then let me show you.' She tapped at the keyboard and brought up pictures of scenery — a foggy day in London from bygone times, a snowscape, a vast ocean with blue and greens so vivid I could feel my eyes react to the intensity, and a rainy day, figures hurrying along a city street, blurred by the rain, sheltering under umbrellas, shadows against the brightly lit shop windows. She pointed to the rainy image and read the caption. '5:30pm on a rainy day in November.'

My heart pounded anxiously. I knew she wanted me to understand but I didn't, and yet she thought I could, that I was capable of looking at things differently.

She spoke calmly. 'Do you see the pictures — or do you sense the atmospheres?'

'I sense the atmospheres — the rain, fog, snow and the sea.'

'Excellent. Now how do we transfer those feelings into a dress?'

'I have no idea.'

'Here's how. A truly beautiful dress, the type we are tasked to make, shouldn't be a specific colour. Oh yes, it would be lovely enough, but to create something with outstanding impact, a lingering impression, we have to evoke a feeling and we do that by combining fabrics, the tones, the textures, the design of the gown, how it flows when it's worn and how it photographs. We must do all these things. And if we do, we'll have done our job to the utmost of our ability.'

My attention was drawn to a silky grey–green fabric on a shelf. The colour wasn't too grey or too green. It was light in colour and in weight. 'That fabric reminds me of sea foam.'

'Bring it down and put it on the table.'

I got up, filled with enthusiasm. I climbed on to a little step ladder and pulled the roll of fabric from the shelf. Beside it was another fabric. 'This one looks like the sea near the harbour.'

I brought it down too, and we began to choose around twenty different fabrics, laying them out on the tables and studying the effects of them next to each other.

'Didn't the Hollywood stylists want to know what colour you planned to make the dresses?' I asked her.

'They did. I told them I don't work that way. They insisted on seeing the actual designs, but they're leaving me to choose the fabrics. My designs are known for this. That's why they came to me.' She showed me the four designs on the screen. All four were full–length evening gowns. A figure–skimming fish tail. A fairytale number. One that dipped low in the back. And an ethereal dress with vintage styling. 'The designs will alter accordingly. I have the exact size requirements.'

'Will you need to go to Hollywood for the final fittings? Or will they come here?'

'No, I prefer having only the measurements. They don't whinge, suggest changes that won't work during fittings when the dress isn't even finished. No, over the years I've kept a distance from my clients and it works.' She then showed me the trailer for the movie. 'It's an international thriller with lots of atmospheric shots and they want me to somehow incorporate those aspects into the designs. London at night, in the snow and rain along with fantastic sea views in San Francisco and the vibrancy of other cities are key elements. The stylists are following their own brief from the director and others involved in the film's marketing and they want the dresses to look part of the promotion.'

Judith brought the tea through. 'Chocolate biscuits are banned in the sewing room, but shortbread is permitted.' She set the tea up on a table near the window and put shortbread petticoat tails on a plate.

'What do you think of some of our fabric choices?' the dressmaker asked Judith. 'We're playing around with ideas.'

Judith studied them and then said, 'I really like those. They look like the colour of the sea down at the harbour shops.'

The dressmaker laughed. 'Well done, Tiree.'

We continued playing around with fabric combinations until it was quite late.

The dressmaker was keen on our choices. 'I like these. They'll work.'

We'd chosen the sea foam combination, shimmering greys and silvery chiffons, gold tulle gleaming like summer sunshine and the richest ambers and bronze crepe de chine and organza.

Ignoring the late hour, the dressmaker folded the sea foam fabric expertly on the cutting tables, laid the five pattern pieces of one of the dresses on top, and pinned them in place. She handed me a pair of scissors. 'Would you care to cut the pieces?'

I accepted the scissors.

Judith sat down out of the way and watched.

I kept my hands steady, took a deep breath and began cutting, enjoying the feel of the scissors slicing through the layers of fabric. I'd always loved this part of the process. The dressmaker had chosen the right person for this type of task. The sewing? Well, I doubted I was up to her standard, but I was prepared to learn from her and bring my own experience into the mix.

'We can do this, Tiree,' the dressmaker said, encouraging me to cut all the pieces out ready for sewing the next day.

Yes, I thought, we can. It'll be hard work but worth it.

Once I was finished, we left the work ready to begin sewing in the morning. The dressmaker flicked the lights off in the sewing room and we went through to the living room.

'You're welcome to stay here overnight if you're not ready to settle into the cottage this evening,' she offered.

'No, I'm fine. I'm looking forward to living in the cottage.'

Judith, I learned, lived further along the coast in the house she'd shared with her late husband. She offered to drive back with me, but I assured her I now knew the way down to the harbour. They packed a bag of groceries for me with fresh milk, bread, tea and biscuits.

The dressmaker walked me to the front door. The cold night air blew in when she opened it. She pulled her cardigan around her.

I stepped outside. 'Did you know I'd accept your offer to come here?' I asked her.

She gave me a knowing smile.

I smiled back and went to walk away.

'What did you think of Tavion?' she said.

'Very pleasant.'

'Hmmm.'

19

I walked over to my car.

'Come up for breakfast,' she said, waving me off. 'And thanks again for cutting the dress.'

I waved back to her. No, I thought, she was the one who had done me the favour, taking a chance on me when few in this world would, or ever had.

Further down the road car headlights shone in the darkness. Another car wanted to drive past, but there wasn't enough room for both of us on the narrow road. The car ahead stopped and I saw the figure of a man walk towards me. It was Tavion. I opened the window to speak to him.

'Did you enjoy your visit to the dressmaker?' he asked.

'I did, thanks.'

'Are you heading back home? Do you want me to lead the way down to the harbour?'

'No, I'm not lost. In fact, I've accepted the dressmaker's apprenticeship offer. I'm staying in the pink cottage. I'm moving in.'

His face lit up. 'That's great. It's always good to have new people join the community. If you're looking to get married, there are plenty of single men around these parts.'

'I'm not here to find a husband. I'm here to work.'

He looked flustered and I think he wished he'd kept his comment to himself. 'No, no, I eh, what I meant was, if you were interested in finding a husband, not me of course, though I am single and unattached, but I'm not suggesting I'd be ideal husband material...'

I watched him dig himself deeper into the doop with every word.

He finally stopped and took a deep breath. 'What I actually mean is, if you're single it's different here than in the city. We've got some fine men for you to fancy.'

My eyes widened.

'No, no, that sounds awful. What I really wanted to say was...' He sighed heavily. 'I've made a complete arse of myself, haven't I?'

I nodded.

He pointed to his car. 'I'll go now. I'll reverse into the bushes and let you drive past.'

I bet he wished he could reverse the things he's just said. I tried not to laugh.

I heard the gears crunch when he put his car into reverse.

I drove by as he cleared the road. I gave him a toot on my horn and laughed to myself. He'd be cringing in his sturdy boots and wondering if I'd tell the dressmaker and Judith. Well, of course I would. Girls secrets and gossip needed to be shared.

I parked outside the cottage, took my things inside and had a look around. The air was cold but fresh, everything recently cleaned. The living room curtains had a strawberry print and the decor was a lovely mix of warm creams and pale pink with dashes of colour, especially on the cushions with their pretty floral prints and butterfly designs. I pictured adding some of my own cushions — a seahorse and pink and blue sewing machines.

I put the milk in the fridge and looked at the empty tables and workspace where the jam making had been. Soon the shelves would be filled with my stash of fabrics, and I'd have my sewing machine set up along with plenty of room for pattern cutting. I sat down on the wooden chair with its blue strawberry cushions and tried the tables out for size. Yes, they were an ideal height for sewing. This could work.

For a moment, just a moment, I wished my mother could be here to share this with me. I hoped she'd be pleased I was back to where we'd first started sewing, in the Highlands with the dressmaker. I never imagined I'd be the dressmaker's apprentice, something my mother had enjoyed all those years ago.

I shook the thoughts from my mind. They only upset me, and I know my mother would never want that. 'Be happy, Tiree,' she used to say when times were hard. 'Smile even though things are difficult. Make the most of what you have because one day it will only be a memory you wished you'd cherished better.' I stood up and took a deep breath. I'd cherish this chance I'd been offered.

Although I could've lit the fire in the living room, I decided to leave it and get ready for bed. The cottage had two bedrooms and I chose the one at the front so I could gaze out at the sea at night. Clean linen had been put on the beds by Judith and the cottage was basically ready for use.

I settled down and looked out at the dark sky and the sea. How quickly things had changed, for the better. I felt a shiver of nervous anticipation thinking about moving away from the city, leaving the flat, packing up and coming to live in a seaside cottage. And sewing to the high standards required by the dressmaker.

21

I fell asleep thinking about all the things I'd have to do and woke up early, filled with enthusiasm, ready to start.

The day was overcast. A wild morning. I tidied myself, dressed warmly and drove up to the dressmaker's cottage for breakfast.

An attractive man in his mid–thirties was talking to Judith at the front door. The breeze gave his light brown hair a fashionably windswept style, or perhaps this was his usual look. Judith smiled when I arrived and the man turned round to acknowledge me.

'This is Tiree,' said Judith. 'We're just arranging with the silversmith to pick up your belongings from the city.'

'I'm happy to drive up this morning,' he said. 'We could be there and back by the late afternoon. Sunday is my least busy day, unless you want to wait until next Sunday.' His eyes, the same light brown as his hair, gazed at me, waiting on an answer.

I hesitated. I'd been expecting breakfast and a bit of sewing, not driving off to pack up my entire life.

Judith prompted me. 'What do you think, Tiree? Big Sam's available today. We could have a quick breakfast while he goes and brings the van up.'

'Eh, yes, great. Let's do it,' I said.

'I'll be back in just over half an hour.' And off he went. He wore dark jeans and a thick jumper the colour of the deep greens of the trees around the cottage. His build lived up to his name, Big Sam. Quite a hunk.

'Come on,' Judith urged me. 'We'll have a cup of tea and toast.' She kept nattering as she swept me through to the kitchen where the dressmaker was seated having her breakfast and checking out the world on her laptop on the kitchen table.

'How did you get on at the cottage?' the dressmaker asked me. 'Did you sleep well?'

'I slept great.'

Judith bustled around, making toast and a fresh pot of tea. 'We emailed Big Sam this morning about picking up your belongings. He's got everything we need — packing cases and storage boxes and strong muscles for lifting the heavy stuff.'

'My flat is three floors up but there's a lift that's usually working.'

'I'll come with you to help you pack,' said Judith. 'I've got a bit of muscle myself.' She jokingly flexed her biceps beneath her woolly cardigan.

I helped myself to a couple of slices of toast with raspberry jam. 'The flat is part furnished so a lot of it isn't even mine. It'll mainly be my plastic storage boxes filled with my fabric stash and items that are precious — things belonging to my mother, things we made.' I'd accumulated numerous storage boxes, so many I'd stacked them into two equal piles. I'd added a makeshift top and used it as a layout table.

The dressmaker put marmalade on her toast. 'You can keep those here. There is plenty of space in the spare rooms. I use them for working.' She smiled to herself. 'From the outside, my cottage looks like a traditional house, but it's really a working home with every room utilised for sewing and dressmaking. You can see the rooms when you get back. I want you to get some breakfast down you before Sam arrives with the van.' She looked at me. 'What did you think of him?'

Again, her question hung in the air, ponderous, as if she knew something.

'He seems very pleasant — and well–named.'

Judith finished eating her toast. 'He's a strapping fella.' She glanced at the dressmaker.

'Don't you two go matchmaking me up with any of the men around here,' I said lightly.

Judith didn't flinch. 'There are a few who are eligible, if you're interested.'

'So I hear.'

They both looked at me.

'Who told you?' Judith asked.

I relayed the things Tavion had said.

'He seems to like you,' said Judith. 'We may have a wee romance in the offing.'

I blushed a little. 'Romance isn't on my agenda. I explained to him I'm here to work.'

'There's always room for romance,' the dressmaker told me. 'Even when we're busy.'

CHAPTER THREE

Cats, Cushions & Fairy Cakes

The peep of a van horn announced the arrival of Big Sam. Judith scurried around, leaving instructions with the dressmaker to heat up the pot of homemade soup she'd prepared earlier, and grabbed her bag and coat.

We hurried out. Sam stood at the passenger door and opened it so we could clamber into the front seat with him.

He revved up the engine. 'Ready to rock and roll ladies?'

We were, though I didn't expect he meant it literally. He adjusted the volume of the lively music emanating from the speakers on the dashboard. Waving to the dressmaker, the three of us set off for the city, singing along to the uplifting tunes.

I sang songs I'd heard over the years but had never uttered. I surprised myself. Judith was happy. Perhaps she'd been in the van before with Sam, and not in a compromising way. The laughter and sing–song made the drive seem a short one, and bolstered my spirits at the prospect of wrapping up my past and leaving it behind.

I'd been right about my storage and fabric stash boxes being the majority of my belongings. If I hadn't felt so relieved that the packing wasn't difficult I might have been rather melancholy. With three sets of enthusiastic hands and two sets of strong muscles, we lifted, shifted and packed my world up and drove off with it. We sang all the way back.

I'd left the keys to the flat with the caretaker of the building and told him I'd email to cancel the lease. He promised to forward any mail to my new address. I'd also emailed the department store, telling my manager I'd accepted the apprenticeship and wouldn't be back to work. I'd forgo a month's rent on the flat, but it was a small price to pay to move to the cottage, and the dressmaker had agreed to pay me a lot more in wages than I earned at the department store. All I had to sort out was my banking and a couple of other details which I could do by email or phone once I moved into the cottage.

When we arrived outside the pink cottage, it felt like I'd stepped into some weird time warp where I'd been in the city and back before it was time for afternoon tea, which we were all gasping for.

The first thing I did was put the kettle on and set the cups up. My throat was parched from singing, laughing and having a good time.

Sam brought in several boxes and bags stuffed with clothes along with my sewing machine, overlocker and cutting table. He put the table in the kitchen. 'I'll take the rest up to the dressmaker's cottage.'

He looked around, cupping his mug of tea. 'This cottage is nice. It smells of strawberries and sweetness.' He smiled at me.

'You probably enjoyed the jam they used to make here. It was sold at the grocery shop and the post office,' said Judith.

'Yes, I did,' he said. 'Will you be making jam, Tiree?'

'No, I'll be sewing.'

'Sewing? Is that what all the boxes of materials and the sewing machines are for?'

'Yes.'

'Tiree is the dressmaker's new apprentice.' We'd been so busy singing we hadn't actually told him the details about why I was moving here.

'Welcome to the community, Tiree. If you ever need any fancy silver buttons for your outfits, let me know.'

'I will,' I said. It was hard to imagine such big, strong hands working with intricate silversmith techniques.

'Sam made the silver Thimble for the collar of the dressmaker's cat,' said Judith.

I'd still to meet the cat.

He downed the rest of his tea and headed out with Judith.

'What about payment?' I whispered to her.

'Don't worry. The dressmaker is taking care of it,' she whispered back. 'Come up for dinner when you're ready.'

After they drove off, I started unpacking things. I set my sewing machine, overlocker and various sewing accessories up in the old jam making area. My cutting table fitted in nicely. Even a rough set up looked inviting. I cleaned and oiled my sewing machine and overlocker, checked they worked, which they did, reliable as ever. It felt strange to hear my sewing machine whirring again after not using it for so long.

Then I hung my clothes in the wardrobes and folded them into the chests of drawers. I figured if I did everything while I was still buzzing with excitement I could get most of it unpacked.

Sam had put my selection of cushions into a packing box. I opened it and arranged the flowery cat with its cheerful face on the comfy chairs along with the fairy cake and button cushions. The sewing machine softies and seahorse cushions went well with the sofa. I sat the patchwork robin and yacht cushions on my bed. I put the brightly coloured diva moth cushion in the kitchen to soften one of the wooden chairs and hung my sewing apron up on the back of the kitchen door.

It didn't take as long as I thought to sort things out. I realised I didn't own a lot of stuff, which was handy for moving but made me wonder if I'd ever be settled in a home of my own. I stood in the living room and listened to how quiet it was. In the city there was constant noise. This was bliss — and it was mine for the next year maybe two years if the dressmaker extended the lease. The past two years had swept by so quickly with everything that had happened. I promised myself I'd treasure the time living in the pretty pink cottage and see where the future took me.

Later, I drove up to the dressmaker's cottage for dinner. Tomorrow I planned to get some fresh groceries in and start cooking for myself.

Judith welcomed me in. 'Perfect timing. The steak pie is ready. Maybe you could make us a pot of tea while I serve it up.'

I was happy to help. The kitchen table was set for three, and the heat from the stove created a cosy atmosphere.

Judith took a large ashet containing the steak pie from the oven. The puff pastry had risen to a light golden crispness. 'The dressmaker's been busy sewing while we were away. She's got the dress you cut sewn together. It looks sensational. You'll see it after dinner.'

The dressmaker came through and sat down.

'I was just telling Tiree about how much of the dress you've sewn.'

'I thought I'd make a start on it while you two were off gallivanting,' she joked.

'I can't wait to see it. Can I have a peek?'

The dressmaker nodded.

Judith drained the pot of potatoes. 'Be quick. Don't let your dinner get cold.'

I hurried through to the sewing room — and there it was. The dress that looked like the sea. I gazed at the work she'd done on it. The mannequin was wearing it. She'd sewn all the main pieces together, though the neckline, hem and other edges still needed work. 'Oh my,' I gasped. I shouted through to them. 'It's fantastic.'

A loud meow sounded from under one of the tables. I jumped, then saw two startling green eyes peer out at me.

'Thimble?'

The cat didn't respond to his name.

I bent down to have a look at him. He was a beautiful black cat with amazing green eyes.

'Tiree, come and get your dinner.'

Not wishing to upset Judith, I hurried back through. A plate of steak pie, potatoes, carrots, peas and lashings of gravy was waiting for me.

'The dress is a winner, isn't it?' said Judith.

'It's gorgeous.'

The dressmaker smiled at me. 'Obviously it needs finishing.'

'Yes,' I said, 'but I love the effect of the fabrics, the way it shimmers in the light. You've made it look like...well, like the sea, fluid. I wish I had your talent, your skills.'

'That's what you're here to learn. I have to say you'd cut it very well. Great cutting is the secret to all well made dresses.' She paused and then said, 'And was that Thimble I heard through there?'

'Yes, he's lovely. He was peering at me from under the table. I saw the Thimble on his collar, the one Sam made.'

Judith offered me more vegetables from the terrine and I accepted them. 'Sam put the rest of your belongings in one of the rooms. He was quite chatty about you, asking all sorts of questions.'

'Including whether or not you were married,' the dressmaker added.

'What is it with men and marriage around here?' I tried not to blush.

'You're blushing,' said the dressmaker.

'It's the heat of the kitchen.'

'No, you're blushing,' she insisted.

They both giggled.

'I have no intention of falling for any man's charms. I just want to be free to enjoy myself and learn how to make dresses even a fraction as beautiful as the one you've sewn.'

'Don't you want to settle down one day?' Judith asked.

'Yes, one day. I've never been lucky when it comes to romance.'

'Well,' said the dressmaker, 'we'll see what happens.'

After dinner I saw where my things were stored — in one of the rooms upstairs. I knew they'd be safe there amid the remnants of fabric and other items for sewing. I wondered where the dressmaker kept her stock of dresses.

'I sell every dress I sew. I make them and sell them.'

We went back downstairs and into the sewing room. Although it was evening, we planned to work on the dress.

'You haven't shown Tiree the book with all the fabric swatches, colour charts and photographs of the dresses you've made,' Judith reminded her. 'Do you want me to bring it through?'

'If you wouldn't mind, Judith.'

Judith went through to the living room and came back lugging an enormous book.

I jumped up. 'Let me give you a hand with it.'

We put it down on the table. In width and breadth it was the size of an A3 poster and as thick as a doorstep. The binding looked ancient, like weather beaten material embossed with leaves and gold leaf effect. It looked like something I'd seen in a fantasy film.

The dressmaker opened it and began showing me the designs — fashion illustrations drawn in pen and ink with washes of watercolour.

'These are exquisite,' I said, thinking they'd make great prints.

'Thank you. I enjoy drawing the designs. I love all parts of the process, but over the years I've accumulated samples of fabrics, colour ranges showing the tones, the hues and what works well together.'

I loved pouring over the array of artwork and ideas, the designs and hundreds of colour swatches, some made from watercolour, others from little pieces of fabric, and all put together into this one book by the dressmaker.

She closed the book and I helped Judith carry it back through to the living room.

'You can study the book whenever you want,' the dressmaker told me, 'but now we must push on with the work.' She went over to one of the tables and it was only then I noticed she'd laid out other fabrics and pinned the pattern pieces on. 'I've a feeling they're going to ask for these dresses a lot sooner than planned. I'd feel happier if all the pieces were cut and ready for sewing. So would you cut those while I get the next dress ready for cutting?'

'Yes.' I took the scissors and carefully cut out the pattern pieces while the dressmaker worked at the other table, folding the fabric and arranging the paper pattern on top.

'When do you think they'll want the dresses?' Judith asked her.

'Soon. I know we're supposed to have several weeks to finish them.' The dressmaker shook her head. 'I just keeping thinking they'll want at least two of them a lot sooner.'

Judith didn't question the dressmaker's hunch. Instead, she helped her fold the fabrics while I got on with the process of cutting.

We finished around midnight. Three dresses were fully cut and ready to be sewn. 'We'll start sewing them tomorrow,' the dressmaker told me. 'We'd all better get some sleep.'

I drove back to the cottage and went straight to bed. What a day it had been, and what an evening. Seeing the dressmaker work was fascinating. I'd expected someone who'd been dressmaking all her life to be skilled and efficient. She certainly was, but I was amazed how quickly she could work.

She showed me her methods for handling the silk and satin without bruising the fabric. And she gave me the offcuts from the dress material when I mentioned they'd make a nice patchwork quilt. Now I had time to think about it, I quite liked the idea of creating a large book of samples and sketches of my own. I fell asleep thinking how I'd make it and listening to the sounds of the sea.

CHAPTER FOUR

Sewing & Romance

The next morning I bought bread, milk, vegetables and other items from the grocery shop a few minutes walk from my cottage. The sea swept along the coast, churned up by the blustery wind. Laden with bags of shopping, I went into the post office and bought several large sheets of white card. I planned to make a book like the dressmaker had, filled with my clothes designs, patterns and fabrics.

The wind whipped off the sea as I headed along to my cottage, tying to keep a hold of the card.

'Let me give you a hand with those before the wind blows you away,' a man said.

'Tavion.'

He grabbed the sheets of card. 'These are like a kite. You'll take off if you're not careful,' he joked.

I was grateful for the help. He scooped two of the bags off me as well and we walked together towards the cottage. Flurries of pink blossom from the cherry trees in the cottage garden suddenly blew all around us.

Tavion smiled as it fell on us and pink petals dappled our clothes. 'Nature's confetti.'

I glanced at him.

'The ladies around here would probably take it as a sign,' he said.

'A sign of what? Oh, right. Confetti.' And I was back to the hint of eligible men and marriage.

I brushed strands of my hair back from my face. 'I underestimated how strong the wind was.' I scrambled in my coat pocket for my keys and unlocked the front door.

We stepped inside and I closed it against the wind. He followed me through to the kitchen and put the bags of shopping down. 'What's all this card for?'

'I'm planning on making a book with lots of scraps of fabric and dress designs.' I explained about the dressmaker's book.

'Sounds interesting.' He laid the sheets of card flat on the table beside my sewing machine.

30

'I used to enjoy scrapbooking.' He didn't seem to know what it was. 'Anyway, this is just like a large scrapbook. Once I have several sheets complete, I'll think about how to bind it. I'll probably put it into some sort of folder.'

'The silversmith does a bit of bookbinding, or so I've heard.'

'Is there anything Sam doesn't do?'

'He doesn't grow flowers.' Tavion brought a small bag of flower bulbs from his jacket pocket. 'I've been looking for an excuse to chap your door.'

'An excuse? You don't need an excuse, Tavion. Just be straightforward.'

'Okay. I did want to give you the bulbs because they're ready for planting and will flower later in the year, but what I really wanted to do was offer you the use of my cottage for your party.'

'What party?' Then it dawned on me. 'Oh the welcoming party. I'm sorry if I've missed the purpose of it. I thought it was a sort of house warming and would be held here.'

'It should. However, this wee cottage isn't made for any more than a handful of guests. Six people in your living will be a crowd. I'm maybe being presumptuous to think I'll be invited. Judith has mentioned that Ethel intends turning up along with several others who are keen to meet you. So that's at least twelve, not including the postmaster or the chocolatier. Then there's Big Sam who by sheer size counts for at least two guests.'

I laughed. 'So what did you have in mind?'

'Have the party at my house. It's got a large lounge that extends out the back. I'm not much use at cooking, so you'll have to help out with the catering. I'm happy to supply cakes and stuff for sandwiches. If any of the other welcoming parties are anything to go by, all the guests will turn up with either home baking or a bottle of the hard stuff.'

'I don't want to put you to any bother, and I'm not sure what my plans will be for the party.'

'Think it over. Let me know if you'd like to use my house. It's no bother at all.'

He left, wishing me luck with creating my sewing book and giving instructions on where to plant the bulbs.

I planted them as he'd suggested. I'd never planted bulbs before and hoped I'd made a good enough job of it.

I made breakfast and then drove up to the dressmaker's cottage. Sunlight flickered through the branches of the trees. The road twisted and turned, and I saw glimpses of the various cottages dotted along the coastline and the patchwork of fields with the sea glistening in the distance. There was something truly magical about living here, and I was glad I'd taken a chance and given up my old life for this.

The dressmaker was already working on machining the seams of one of the dresses — the gold tulle did indeed gleam like summer sunshine. Fit for a fairytale princess or a Hollywood star who needed to shine at the movie premiere.

I settled down to help her and we chatted while we worked. I told her about Tavion's offer. Judith joined in the conversation.

'Tavion's cottage is similar in size to this one. It's certainly got adequate room for the party,' said Judith.

The dressmaker nodded. 'I'd take him up on his offer. Your cottage is a bit small for a proper party.'

'When do you think I should have the party?'

'Later this week,' the dressmaker suggested. 'Ask Tavion if it suits him. A few days notice is all people need to bake cakes or make things for you. It's all part of the welcoming.'

'People are relieved the dressmaker has taken on the cottage lease,' said Judith. 'When we lost the jam making, people around here were worried the cottage would be undone, changed into something that doesn't fit in, so they're very happy it's going to be cherished almost as it was. And be prepared to have all those who love to sew bombarding you with questions about what you're learning from the dressmaker. They've lost a jam–maker but gained a new dressmaker's apprentice.'

'I'll speak to Tavion later today and get things organised,' I said, pinning the bodice of a dress. The amber and bronze crepe de chine worked so well with the organza layers of the skirt.

We stopped for a light lunch and then continued sewing throughout the afternoon. We chatted while we sewed and the hours flew by. It was only when I noticed it was starting to become dark outside that I realised the time.

'I think you've done enough,' the dressmaker said to me. 'We've made superb progress with the dresses.'

'You're welcome to stay for dinner,' Judith offered.

'Thanks, but I think I'll head back. I bought shopping in this morning and I want to sort out the rest of the unpacking and organising my sewing room.'

They waved me off, and on the way back I decided to pull over and give Tavion a call.

'I'd like to take you up on your offer.'

'Brilliant. When were you thinking of having the party?'

'A few days from now.'

'Any time suits me,' Then he said, 'Where are you?'

'I'm on my way home. I've been dressmaking all day.'

'Do you want to drop by for a few minutes to see the house? It would give you a better idea of what you're letting yourself in for.'

He was joking, but it did make me wonder.

'My house isn't far from the dressmaker's cottage.'

'I'm at the narrow part of the road where you reversed to let me by.'

'Hang on. I'll be there in a few minutes.'

I clicked the phone off and waited. Several minutes later his car headlights shone on the road. I flashed my lights, signalling I'd follow him and he led the way to his house.

It was similar in size to the dressmaker's cottage but a different style, very open and built from grey stone. Although he had a substantial garden, his two–storey cottage faced the fields he owned. From the top window he probably had a view of the harbour, definitely the sea in the distance and a wide area of cultivated fields growing flowers.

We parked in the driveway and he led me inside the house.

There was nothing chintz or flowery about it. Calming blues and neutral tones dominated the colour scheme, and it had an airy quality to it. Nothing fussy. No frills. And it was tidy.

'I have a housekeeper who comes in once or twice a week,' he said, as if reading my thoughts. 'I'm not particularly domesticated, though I do like being at home.'

He led me through to the lounge. 'This is where I thought you could have the party. It leads on to the kitchen and extends through to the patio.'

Logs burned in the large fireplace and the blue and beige coloured rugs matched the sofas and chairs. Lamps provided soft lighting and the furniture looked like it had been polished that day. A vase of flowers sat on the old–fashioned sideboard, the only floral hint in the entire room. Two seascape paintings hung on the walls, and apart from a bookcase filled with botanical books there was no ornamentation.

I liked it.

I walked the length of the room and looked out at the view through the patio windows and doors. The flower fields stretched all around, mainly daffodils and tulips.

'The view is a lot more colourful in the summer when the ranges of flowers are at their height.'

I imagined it would be, but it was lovely now. I felt myself relax just looking at it. Tavion caused the opposite effect, especially when he stood beside me, tall and manly, pointing out where the harvests of flowers were due and the work involved. He also explained that he gave talks about his work.

'It sounds fascinating, and a lot of hard work,' I said, trying to keep my voice steady. He wore an Aran jumper and snug–fitting navy cords. For the first time in ages I was aware of a masculine presence, as if I'd suddenly looked up from the depths of a long winter to see a lighter side of my surroundings.

'It's both, but I love my work. I was brought up by my father to be a flower grower. After he died, I inherited the property and the land to cultivate.'

He'd obviously done well for himself and I appreciated the offer to hold my party here.

'Would you like to stay for dinner?' he said. 'I'm not having anything special. I was about to throw a pizza in the oven when you phoned.'

'Oh, I eh...'

'The pizza's too large for one. You'd be doing me a favour, saving me eating the other portion for supper later tonight.' He smiled. He had such a charming smile mixed with raw masculinity. My stomach knotted with a flicker of desire, or nervousness, perhaps both.

He strode through to the kitchen. 'Pizza going in now. Gas Mark pot luck, somewhere round about the middle bit of the dial should cook it without burning.'

I laughed and followed him through. The kitchen was blue and white with a pale wooden table in the centre. I hung my jacket over the back of a chair. The kitchen felt quite warm. Tavion pushed up the sleeves of his jumper to reveal his muscled forearms, honed from years of working at his trade. His shoulders were broad, and even in the sizeable kitchen he dominated the space.

'Any volunteers to set the table would be great.' He checked a pot of simmering mixed vegetables on the stove.

I laid the plates and cutlery on the table while Tavion barged around the kitchen. I think he was as nervous as me.

'Bottle of wine, tea or coffee?' he offered.

'Tea for me.'

'Me too.'

I giggled when I saw the cosy on this teapot. It was bright yellow and covered with knitted flowers and butterflies. Although pretty, it seemed out of place in his strong hands.

'Don't laugh,' he said trying to keep a straight face. 'Judith knitted this for me for Christmas.'

'It's lovely. Really it is.'

He dropped teabags into the pot before pulling the flowery cosy on again. 'It's actually very practical and keeps the tea warm.' He held it up to show me how the butterflies were attached to the top so that they wobbled as if flying around the flowers. 'Judith will probably knit a tea cosy for you.'

'I love things like that.'

He checked on the pizza. 'What else do you love? Tell me a bit about yourself apart from the things I know.' He listed some of things. 'I know you're from the city, you're the dressmaker's new apprentice, you're living in the pink cottage, you're planning on making an enormous fabric scrapbook, you like pizza, prefer tea to wine and love tea cosies.' He grinned at me. 'So what else?'

'I like sewing cushions with fancy designs.'

'Ah, the flowery cats and sewing machine cushions. I saw those. Very pretty.'

'I have other designs in my bedroom.' The words were out before I realised how it sounded. 'Not that you'll ever see those. I mean, you won't be in my bedroom.'

Tavion guffawed.

My face burned with embarrassment.

He took sea salt and black pepper from the cupboard and held up a condiment jar. 'Beetroot?'

He couldn't stop laughing and this made me laugh, and somehow any nervousness faded as we worked together to serve up the pizza, vegetables and tea.

We sat down at the table and chatted until I made another pot of tea, admiring Judith's handiwork. I wished I could knit butterflies like hers.

From the kitchen window I saw storm clouds descending over the fields. 'It looks like a thunder storm is on its way. I'd better get back. Thanks for dinner.'

'And thank you for the company. I'll have everything ready for your party. We'll organise it between us. Let me know if I need to sort out anything in particular. I'll let people know there's a party and try to keep a tab on the numbers.'

He showed me to the front door and I stood for a moment gazing out at the fields and a cottage further along in the distance.

'That's the beemaster's cottage. Bredon's my nearest neighbour. He's away on business. I'll introduce you when he gets back. He's eh...quite popular with the ladies.'

'Is he now?'

'Not that he's a flirt or anything like that. The women think he's handsome and he has a tendency to cause a few hearts around here to flutter.'

'So he's single?'

'He is. And so am I. Just saying.' He grinned.

I smiled back at him and tried not to feel the need to give him a huge hug. 'Thanks again, Tavion.' I hurried to my car and drove off, hoping I'd get back before the rain started.

A thunder and lightning storm tore across the sky.

I sat at the front window in the living room, peering out from behind the strawberry curtains. The flashes lit up the sea, and I was glad to be cosy inside the cottage, sipping a late night cup of broth and wondering why I couldn't get the sense of Tavion out of my thoughts.

I'd enjoyed his company. When he looked at me with his hazel eyes he made me feel as if he was interested in me, in the things I liked and what I was hoping to achieve. It was a welcome change from my boyfriends in the past who had no interest in my sewing or thought it was a frivolous pastime. Tavion noticed the small things, such as the cushions, which were important to me. I liked that. I liked Tavion.

Maybe it was the storm that unsettled me. I didn't feel tired even though it was late. I decided to rummage through my fabric stash and stick little pieces of my favourites on to the first two sheets of card. The start of the book. I included a scrap of herringbone, remembering the waistcoat I'd made. I had a waistcoat pattern I'd designed and used lots of times. I loved waistcoats, wearing them and sewing them. I intended added sketches to accompany the fabrics. I also added pieces of the offcuts the dressmaker had given me from the Hollywood dresses. I tucked the remainder of the offcuts in a bag, intending to sew them into a quilt.

Finally, I tidied my sewing scraps away and went to bed while the storm raged around the cottage.

By morning the only sign left of the storm was a blustery wind and pieces of seaweed washed up by the waves hitting off the harbour wall. I stepped outside and filled my lungs with the salty fresh air. It gave me an appetite for breakfast and an invigorating start to another busy sewing day.

The dressmaker and Judith were bustling around when I arrived for work.

'I was right about them wanting the dresses sooner than planned,' the dressmaker said to me. 'I got up this morning to an email from them asking me to send one of the dresses, though preferably two, as soon as possible. They want them for photographs for promotional posters.'

I took my coat off and put my bag down. 'Did they say which ones they want first?'

'Yes.' The dressmaker worked on one of the dresses while we spoke — the sea dress. 'Thankfully, it's this one which I'll have finished by this afternoon and that one over there.' She pointed to the fairytale gown draped around a mannequin. 'So I need you to concentrate on finishing the organza hemline and adding the beading to the bodice.'

'I'll get started on it right away.'

We worked like crazy all morning, stopped for a quick lunch which Judith prepared, then pushed on with finishing the dresses.

'I'm so glad you're here, Tiree,' the dressmaker said while expertly adding a scattering of crystal beading to her dress. The crystals sparkled and looked like flashes of starlight.

'I've phoned the postmaster,' said Judith. 'He's sending someone up late afternoon to pick up the dresses. He says they'll arrive in time at the airport to catch the earliest flight over to Los Angeles.'

I saw the dressmaker's shoulders relax slightly. 'Thanks, Judith.'

I finished the final stitches, pressed the seams and hem very carefully, then I hung it up ready for the dressmaker to check the details. She'd been checking everything I stitched and giving me precise instruction as we sewed.

'This is first–class work, Tiree. I'm delighted with it.' She double–checked the measurements of the dress with the details on her laptop. 'Perfect. We're done.'

The dressmaker folded and packed the dresses into specially designed boxes, adding layers of tissue paper to avoid creasing the fabric.

Judith put them into another box and stuck the address labels on. A process they'd obviously done many times.

The box was picked up, as promised, and taken down to the postmaster. Only then did I feel I could breath. My tidy ponytail was askew and I looked totally drained.

'It's not usually so stressful,' the dressmaker assured me.

'We all look like we've been through a wind tunnel,' said Judith. 'And I haven't sewn anything, but watching you two stitch against the clock is exhausting, and I'm worried I'll spill tea on the dresses or muck them up. I'm always relieved when they're out the door and on their way to the post office.'

I put my coat on and got ready to leave. I'd told them earlier about having had dinner with Tavion the previous night and they'd been teasing me about it as we worked.

'Any dinner date planned this evening with Tavion?' Judith asked.

'No, I'm heading straight home and behaving myself.'

'That's no fun,' said Judith.

'I'm planning on sewing a wraparound skirt, and that's all the fun I'll need tonight.'

The dressmaker reached into her pattern files. 'Do you have a pattern for the skirt?'

'Just a basic one. I've used it before. I found a piece of fabric in my stash last night and thought I'd make a skirt.'

'Trying sewing this one.' The dressmaker handed me one of her own patterns. 'It's a bit more complicated, but I think the finished result is worth it. It sits well around the waist and is a flattering shape over the hips. And help yourself to any of the fabric here.' She pulled down a bolt of exquisite fabric. 'This would work.'

'Oh that's so expensive.' I ran my hand longingly over the material. The design was a modern classic in fabulous shades of blue. I pictured how amazing it would look on a summer's day and yet would transfer well with a cosy jumper and boots for a brisk day.

'Cut three or four metres,' the dressmaker insisted. 'You only need one or two depending on the length to make the skirt, but this will give you extra for good measure.'

I hesitated, and she began to unravel the bolt, measuring out the fabric. She tugged one thread across the width of it to create a marker for a straight line. Then she lifted a pair of scissors and cut it. I noticed her hands were less fragile in their movements. 'There you go,' she said, folding it up and tucking it into my bag.

'Thank you. I'll start on this tonight.'

'Unless Tavion comes chapping on your door with a better offer,' she said teasing me. 'There's always time to sew a skirt, but you have to make time for romance.'

Later that night after I'd cooked dinner, I wondered if I could combine both. I had a few nights to sew the skirt before the party at Tavion's house. I knew I could finish it in time. It would be lovely to wear it to the party with a silky white blouse.

I sewed until the early hours of the morning, enjoying working with the fabric. The dressmaker's pattern was wonderful.

I put my sewing away for the night and knew I'd finish the hem the following evening.

I lay in bed thinking about what I'd bake for the party. A shop bought cake wouldn't do. I'd always liked baking a Victoria daisy cake and decided I'd bake that along with plenty of fairy cakes — chocolate, buttercream and vanilla. Somehow it seemed appropriate to include strawberry fairy cakes — a nod to the strawberry jam cottage that made me feel at home.

CHAPTER FIVE

Fairy Dolls & Dancing

I iced the last fondant daisy on to the Victoria sponge and placed the cake carefully in a box. I carried it to my car and sat it on the back seat along with a humongous number of fairy cakes, and drove to Tavion's house.

The days had zipped by so quickly in a haze of sewing with the dressmaker, finishing my skirt, which I wore as planned, and baking. I'd phoned Tavion each day, organising things, and promised to arrive an hour before the guests were due. However, there were several cars parked outside his house when I pulled up in the driveway and I heard music and laughter drifting from the open doorway. The party had started. I was quite glad. I hadn't fancied hanging around wondering if anyone was going to arrive on time.

I carried the first box of cakes inside and was waylaid several times as Tavion, who was very smartly dressed in dark trousers and a dark shirt, introduced me to people.

'You've just missed the chocolatier,' Tavion told me. 'He dropped off a large chocolate cake, but he had to dash away to deal with his business in the city. He's got a shop there.'

The lounge was quite busy with guests. Tavion introduced me to one of the ladies who was standing beside the postmaster sipping a glass of sherry.

'You already know the postmaster, but this is Ethel. She owns the blue cottage I mentioned to you. Ethel spins and dyes her own yarn.' Tavion relieved me of the cakes and hurried away with them to the kitchen.

'There are more cakes in the car,' I called to him.

'I'll bring them in,' he called back.

Ethel smiled at me, studying my face, as if searching for the little girl she used to know. Her silvery hair was pinned up in a bun and she wore a navy blue dress and cardigan.

'I never thought I'd see you again, Tiree.' She clasped my hands in hers. 'It's wonderful that you're back home after all these years.'

I suddenly felt quite overcome. Her welcome was so genuine. I guess I'd been accustomed to the rough end of the stick for so long in the city, that even with the kindness shown to me by the dressmaker, Judith and Tavion, I was still taken aback by her delight at seeing me. And yes, I remembered her. She saw the recognition in my face and tears welled up in her eyes.

'I remember you, Ethel. Of all the people, your face, your smile and laughter have stayed with me while I grew up.'

We chatted and giggled and I felt totally comfortable with her. She gave me a hand knitted shrug as a welcoming present. I put it on over my white blouse and it fitted well. The yarn had sparkle in it and I loved it.

'You'll have to come and have tea at my cottage,' she said. 'Drop by any time.'

'I'll do that. I'd love to see the yarns you make. They sound brilliant.'

'They *are* brilliant,' a woman around the same age as myself confirmed. She had wide blue eyes, an extremely pretty face, petite build and long strawberry blonde hair plaited and pinned up with butterfly clasps.

Ethel introduced us. 'This is Ione.'

Ione handed me a handmade tote bag with a fairy appliqué on the front and two beautiful hand sewn fairy dolls in it. 'Welcome, Tiree. I hope you like fairies. I sew them with my aunty.' She spoke fast, nervous. 'I wasn't sure what type of fairy doll you'd like so I've chosen two — a patchwork fairy and Daisy Fleabane. People sit them up and use them like cushions. They're part of our home furnishings range.'

The patchwork doll was made from several different flower and fairy print fabrics and included strawberries which I thought was such a personal touch. Daisy Fleabane comprised of white and yellow daisy print material, and they were both so lovely I wouldn't have known which one to choose.

The blue of Ione's eyes was almost turquoise and a fair match for those of Daisy Fleabane. She looked at me expectantly.

'I love fairies. I love rag dolls and these are really beautiful. Thank you, Ione.'

Only then did she relax. 'Everyone's talking about you coming here. How exciting to just leave the city and start a new life at the cottage.'

I nodded. 'It's been a whirlwind and I've still to sort out a few things, but I decided to take a chance to up sticks and make a fresh start. My mother was my best friend and it's as if I'm doing something she would've loved for me — to be the dressmaker's apprentice, as she used to be.' I glanced at Ethel. 'Although I have acquaintances in the city, that's really all they are. My mum and I were close and when I lost her...well...'

'Judith said you lived in a flat and worked in a department store,' said Ethel, seeking to confirm the rumours that were no doubt circulating about my background.

'Yes. I worked with my mother before that. We made dresses and other clothes and household items that we sold online.' I shook my head. 'But I couldn't face doing it on my own and got a job at the department store. However, I recently had my hours cut and a threat of redundancy. I'd also been passed over for promotion so...I decided to make the jump. And here I am. It really has been a whirlwind.'

Tavion overheard us. 'Speaking of whirlwinds, Tiree, there's one in the kitchen right now. And it's me. Is there any chance of a hand to serve up the sandwiches and cakes?'

I pointed at him. 'You've got buttercream on your nose.'

He looked guilty. 'I was eh...just testing the fairy cakes.'

We laughed and I hurried after him to help with the kitchen turmoil. Ethel and Ione insisted on helping, so too did a couple of the other ladies who were keen to hear all about the things I was learning from the dressmaker.

Overrun by women chatting about the ideal way to sew dress darts and insert an invisible zip, Tavion sidled out of the kitchen and made sure the music wasn't tampered with by Big Sam who wanted something more upbeat, more rock and roll.

'We'll rock and roll once everyone has given Tiree her gifts and had something to eat,' Tavion told him.

Judith arrived. The dressmaker wasn't coming to the party. She really did spend most of her time at her cottage. Judith handed me a gift bag. 'You said you liked Tavion's tea cosy so I've knitted one specially for you.'

I peeked inside the bag and there was a knitted pink tea cosy with a strawberry on top.

'Oh it's perfect, Judith. Thank you. It's ideal for the cottage.'

Judith gave me a hug. 'And thank you for all the hard work you've put in helping the dressmaker get those dresses off to Hollywood in time. Sometimes I wish she only made the dresses like she used to. No hassle, no deadlines.' She sighed. 'But Hollywood is where the big bucks are and so the price is a wee bit of pandemonium now and then.'

'Will they let you know when the dresses arrive?' I asked.

'Yes. And she's been contacted by a film company about making a couple of vintage dresses for a period drama that's going to be filmed in the UK. She's considering whether it's worth the bother, but now she's got you to help her, I think she'll take them up on their offer.'

'Sew dresses for the actual film?' I said.

'Wow,' murmured Ione. 'Imagine seeing the things you'd sewn in a film.'

'We'll all have to get together and have a sewing afternoon or evening,' Ethel suggested.

I agreed. 'How about one at my cottage? I'm going to be busy during the day, but we could have a sewing bee in the evening. The cottage is small, but it's not like having a party. We won't be dancing and having a buffet. We'll be sewing.'

'A sewing bee,' said Ethel. 'Let's do it.'

'Yes,' I said. 'It'll be fun.'

'Are knitters welcome?' Judith asked sheepishly.

'Of course,' I said. 'How about three nights from now?'

A few other ladies from the party, including Hilda who was a quilter, expressed their interest in attending the sewing bee evening. At a rough count there would be twelve of us. I planned to use the living room and the sewing room in the kitchen. Cost of entry was some home baking and a love for all things hand made.

'Can I bring my aunty?' Ione asked. 'She's brilliant at sewing. I learned everything I know from her.'

'Your aunty would be very welcome,' I told her. 'I've got my sewing machine and overlocker set up, and a stash of fabrics and threads we can share.'

'I'll bring my patchwork rag doll and fairy doll patterns, and we've a ton of fabric pieces people can use,' said Ione.

'When I tell the dressmaker,' said Judith, 'I'm sure she'll want to contribute some fabric into the mix.'

That sold it. Everyone was in. The sewing bee by the sea was going to be a very busy bee indeed.

'What's all the squeals and giggling about?' Tavion asked. 'Talking about men?'

'No,' said Ethel. 'We're chatting about sewing. Men are interesting creatures, but there's nothing quite like getting together for a sewing bee night.'

'Are men allowed?' the silversmith asked.

Ethel looked up at him. 'Oh don't tell me you can sew or knit as well as everything else you do.'

'No, but I'm keen to learn. I once sewed a button on my shirt. It lasted a whole day before it fell off.' There was a hint of triumph in his tone.

Tavion shook his head. 'I feel obliged to join in, if only to make sure Sam behaves himself.' Then he added, 'It's like letting a cock into the hen house.'

There was a gasp followed by guffaws.

Tavion realised his faux pas. 'I didn't mean cock in the sense of a man's...' His face burned with embarrassment.

All we did was laugh.

'How about some of your rock and roll music now?' Tavion said to Sam.

The two men hurried away, relieved to avoid us poking fun at them.

Fun was definitely on the party's agenda. My face was sore from smiling and laughing. Ione snapped lots of photographs. Everyone gave me gifts or brought home baking. It was the best welcome I'd ever had.

Along with the two fairy dolls, Ione had popped a little bee softie in the bag. I was admiring it when she came over and sat beside me. Big Sam had been whirling her around the dance floor and her tidy pleats now had strands of hair dangling down.

'This is nice.' I held up the little bee.

'I'll show you how I sew them if you like at the sewing bee.'

I nodded. 'I'd like that.'

'Tavion seems taken with you,' she said quietly.

'He's been very kind.'

She gave me a knowing smile. 'I think he fancies you. I can always tell.'

I smiled.

'He's handsome,' she said. 'A few of the men around here are very attractive.'

I could tell from her manner she was referring to someone in particular. 'Who is it you like?'

She shrugged. 'He's not interested in me.'

'Is it someone I've met?'

'No, he's away on business.'

'The flower hunter? I heard he goes away a lot?'

'No, not the flower hunter, though he's totally gorgeous, but I think he's spoken for now. It's early days, but there are rumours he likes a woman who moved here recently.'

'So who is he?'

Wide blue eyes looked to see if anyone was listening. 'The beemaster,' she whispered.

'Tavion told me he's popular with the ladies.'

'He is, though he doesn't have time it seems for anything other than his bees.'

Tavion headed over to us. 'If I have to boogie to one more rock and roll number, I won't be fit for working in my fields tomorrow.' He held out his hand to me. 'If I change the music to a waltz, will you dance with me?'

'How could I refuse?'

Tavion changed the music, and we began waltzing together. Lots of others joined in. I think everyone was glad of the slower pace. The last I saw of Sam he was waltzing Judith around while Ethel danced with the postmaster.

Tavion may have changed the music, but he'd also changed how I felt about him. As he held me in his arms and we danced around the space he'd cleared in his living room, I longed for the song to continue, to feel his manly embrace.

'Is that the skirt you were talking about making?' He glanced down at what I was wearing.

'Yes. The dressmaker gave me a pattern and the fabric.'

'She's a kind person.'

'She is.'

He held me close and we waltzed into the patio area, and for a moment it felt as if we were alone. I glanced out at the fields and the clear, dark sky as we danced.

'Does the dressmaker think you'll settle here?' he asked.

'I don't know. We haven't discussed anything other than the two year apprenticeship.'

'Then supposedly you'd go back to the city and use the skills you'd learned from her to set up your own dressmaking and design business?'

'I suppose so.' I tensed at the thought of leaving and going back to start over yet again.

'Relax,' he murmured reassuringly, feeling the tension in me. He pulled me closer and we slow danced in the patio.

'I love the cottage, and it's so easy to forget I'm only there temporarily. It's long enough but...nothing in my life is ever settled. I'm always making do. I wish I had somewhere less temporary.'

'Perhaps you will.' He gazed down at me. We continued dancing as he spoke quietly. 'When I was younger I used to envy Fintry the flower hunter. He lived with his father who was also a flower hunter. I asked his father to teach me how to be a flower hunter. It sounded so adventurous. I knew about flowers and wanted to sail off with them sometimes when they went abroad. They used to be away for weeks, for months, scouring far flung corners of the world for new species of flowers.'

'Did they ever take you with them?'

'No. Now I'm glad because Fintry's father lives in the Azores, still not quite settled, and Fintry is away again, so his life is always on the go. He's leased out his cottage to a woman, Mairead. She's very nice.'

'You like her?'

He nodded. 'Yes, but we're just friends. Mairead's not for me. She's like you. She's from the city. Mairead's living in the flower hunter's cottage for a year. She moved here in January. She's an artist and sews quilts, and might go to your sewing bee. Though she's kept busy with her work, and she has to tend the flower hunter's garden. That's quite a responsibility. It's a heritage garden.'

'So Mairead isn't going to be here permanently either?'

'No. Not unless she marries the flower hunter. Judith said the dressmaker hinted of a romance between the two of them.'

'Is there canoodling going on here?' Sam asked.

'We're just dancing.'

'I have to be heading home. I wondered if I could have a dance with Tiree before I go.'

Tavion let me go.

I smiled at Tavion and waltzed with Sam before he left. A few people were beginning to leave. The night had been a success.

'I'll help you tidy things before I go,' I said to Tavion.

Judith helped too.

After clearing things away, I left with Judith. Tavion stood at the door of his house and waved to us. Judith drove off to her house and I headed down to my cottage with lots of presents piled in the back seat.

I carried them inside. Sam had given me a silver Thimble he'd inscribed with my name and I placed it carefully in my sewing basket. Hilda made and sold quilts and had given me a quilted cover for my sewing machine that looked like a patchwork cottage. I put the fairy dolls on the window ledges of the living room. They were too pretty to use as cushions. I arranged the bouquet of flowers from Tavion in a couple of vases. The fragrance from the roses and sweet peas filled the living room. I was still wearing the shrug Ethel had knitted for me. I took it off and hung it up in the wardrobe then got ready for bed.

I was looking forward to having the sewing bee. I liked Ethel, Ione, Hilda and the other ladies I'd met. And yet...it was Tavion I thought about as I gazed out at the sea. I could still feel the sense of his arms around me even now. I remembered what Judith had said. 'Love carefully.' I intended to. It would be easy to fall for a man like him. Too easy. I would keep things friendly and be careful not to end up with a broken heart.

CHAPTER SIX

The Sewing Bee

During the next few days I worked hard to help with the dresses —
and I made time to explore the coastline in the early mornings before
work and in the evenings. I went for brisk walks along the shore. I
felt fitter than I had recently in the city. Life had worn me down a
little and now I had a chance to buck myself back up.

To have such a beautiful landscape right outside my cottage was
great. Yes, there were days when the wind was cold and blustery, but
there were times when I felt the warmth of the sun, a hint of summer.

'Getting some air about you?' a man said.

I turned to see Sam smiling at me.

'It's so lovely here.'

He looked up at the sky. 'A fair wind today but it's starting to
feel more summery.'

'Does it get busy in the summer?'

'A wee bit, but we don't have enough shops to keep the tourists
happy, so we're never that busy which suits most of the locals just
fine.' He looked over towards my cottage. 'Settling in okay?'

'Yes, I'm having a sewing bee tonight.'

'Don't worry. I won't be poking my nose in. I'll leave the sewing
to your bee members. You could be quite busy. Glen might even turn
up.'

'Glen?'

'Ethel's granddaughter.'

'I didn't realise her granddaughter stayed with her.'

'She doesn't. Glen lives in the city. She's studying something to
do with textiles and fashion. I'm not really sure. And she does
modelling. She's quite a beauty. Ask Ethel, or Tavion. He's the one
who is sweet on her.'

'On Glen?'

He nodded, causing a wave of disappointment to wash over me.

'No one has even mentioned Glen to me.' I tried not to sound
bitter.

'She's hardly ever here. She keeps promising Ethel she'll visit and then cancels. Ethel thinks the world of her, but personally I think Glen is spoiled and doesn't think twice about letting Ethel down.'

The toot of a horn distracted Sam. 'Sorry, I have to run. See you around, Tiree.'

And off he went, leaving me feeling flattened.

Love carefully. The warning drilled a hole through my heart.

'You're very quiet today,' the dressmaker said as we worked on the sewing.

'Are you okay?' Judith asked. 'Fancy a cup of tea?'

'I wouldn't mind, thanks.'

Judith gave the dressmaker a look and went away to make the tea.

'What's wrong, Tiree?'

'I met Sam today. He told me about Glen.'

The dressmaker's expression showed she knew what I meant.

'He said that Glen could turn up at the sewing bee tonight. He also said that Tavion is sweet on her. Is this true?'

She sighed heavily. 'Perhaps it is. Perhaps not.'

'That's not really an answer.'

'Ethel wants me to teach my skills to Glen.'

'So she is coming here?'

'Probably. She always cancels. She didn't even turn up to Ethel's birthday party in February after making her think she'd be there. She's supposed to be coming here when she finishes her studies. I'm assuming it'll be for the summer, but knowing Glen, she could cancel that too.'

'Are you going to teach her? Will she become another apprentice?'

'No.' The dressmaker sounded adamant. 'Glen only cares about Glen. I've no time for someone who can't see by themselves. Besides, Glen appears to have dress designing talent, but I'm not particularly impressed from the designs I've seen. She's okay, but not like you. You have more talent than Glen will ever have.'

I hadn't expected her to say this. I didn't know what to say. I listened as she continued to tell me about Glen and Tavion.

'He was hung up on her for a while, especially a couple of years ago. Now I think he's realised she's never going to look twice at him. She's too selfish to know how good he would be.'

Judith brought the tea through. I knew she'd overheard the conversation.

'Why didn't either of you tell me about Glen?' I said. 'I assumed Tavion was unattached.'

'He is,' the dressmaker said firmly. 'I decided not to mention Glen because she continues to upset things here from afar without hardly ever setting foot in Ethel's cottage. It's not right that we have to include her in things when she deliberately avoids this community.'

I nodded and sipped my tea.

Judith shook her head. 'Glen is nothing but trouble. It's not that she's a bad person. She's not. She's just very thoughtless.'

'A selfish girl,' the dressmaker muttered. 'She's extremely confident and ambitious and I don't fault her for that. I just resent her attitude. And I mean it when I say she doesn't have as much talent as you do, Tiree.'

'That's very kind of you,' I said quietly.

'Are you upset because you have feelings for Tavion?' Judith asked me.

I gazed into my cup and sighed. 'You warned me, Judith. And I took in your warning. I haven't fallen for Tavion but I do like him and I'm sort of holding back from taking things further.'

Judith leaned forward and spoke softly. 'Don't miss out on any chance of romance because of Glen, or because I told you to love carefully. All I meant was, don't give your trust easily.'

'I don't intend to.'

Judith looked at the dressmaker. 'What do you feel about Tavion? Do you sense things would be better if Tiree stepped back from any involvement with him?'

'My feelings are as they were when Tiree first arrived. When I saw Tavion and his reaction that evening he led you up here, I sensed a possibility between the two of you. I still do. But maybe time is what's needed. Time to settle yourself into the life here before adding romance to the mix.'

Judith broke her biscuit in two. 'Love is never easy, is it?'

We all agreed on that.

I was glad we'd talked things over. I didn't feel so hurt. I also didn't feel let down by Tavion. Everyone had a past love in their life, even if it came to nothing more than longing from afar. I could hardly expect him not to have loved before. But I would be wary and takes things at a slower pace to see how I felt about him over the coming weeks.

I lit the fire in the living room to make the cottage cosy and welcoming for the sewing bee ladies. They were due to arrive at 7:00pm. I'd baked a vanilla sponge and iced cherry cakes and had the cups ready to make the tea and coffee.

Ethel was the first to arrive. 'I brought a fruit cake.'

I took her coat and led her through to the living room.

'You've got the cottage looking lovely,' she said.

'Thanks, Ethel. I eh...I was wondering if I could ask you something. Is Glen coming here?'

'Glen? No, she said she wanted to, but had to work on her fashion studies.'

I gave a tight–lipped smile.

'What is it?'

'Nothing.'

'Is it about Glen and Tavion?'

'Did someone tell you?'

'Judith phoned, but don't concern yourself about Glen. She's never going to date Tavion. She's not interested in him.'

'I understand that, but...' I sighed.

'Tavion's at an age when I think he'd like to settle down. It's reasonable he'd show an interest in you. You're lovely, single and living here now. My advice is to follow your heart, but take care not to fall in love too quickly.'

'Are you there, Tiree?' Hilda called to me.

I hurried through and welcomed Hilda and Ione in along with three other ladies who were all carrying bags of sewing ready to enjoy the bee.

Thankfully, there was no more talk of Glen. We chatted about fabrics, patterns, dresses and designs.

Ethel helped me make the tea and all the ladies chattered and showed each other what they were sewing or hoped to make. And

51

Judith brought her knitting. She was knitting a tea cosy and chatted about the yarn to Ethel.

'What do you do at the dressmaker's cottage?' one of the ladies asked eagerly.

'Yes,' said Hilda. 'Has she taught you anything you could show us?'

I shared tips I'd learned from the dressmaker — how she sewed dress darts, applied beads around a neckline, hemmed chiffon — and let them try out the techniques on pieces of scrap fabric.

I also showed them how to do needleturn appliqué. 'I use this technique for my quilts.'

'I'm a quilter,' said Hilda. 'I'd like to make dresses and skirts that have a flattering fit. I've run a few skirts up on my sewing machine, but they never feel great. I'd like to ask for your tips on how to sew them.'

'I've got a pattern for a wraparound skirt. The dressmaker said I could share it with you,' I said to them.

Judith nodded. 'And the dressmaker gave me a bag full of fabric you can use. It's through in the living room.'

The ladies shared out the fabric and I showed them how to cut out the pattern pieces. Then the whirring of the sewing machines began. A couple of ladies had brought sewing machines with them and we set them up in my sewing room. Everyone helped each other which was the whole purpose of the sewing bee.

Ione had several of her fairy doll designs with her. She showed us a handy method for stuffing the dolls and how to sew the gap shut using a ladder stitch. This created a neat finish to the dolls.

Hilda was an expert quilter and showed a couple of the ladies, including Ione, how she stitched the edges of her quilts and applied the binding.

'I'm going to have a go at making little quilts at home for my fairy dolls,' Ione said to Hilda. 'The finish on my quilts never looks right. I love the way you do it. I'm definitely going to have a go.'

The first hour flew by in a haze of fabric cutting, using my sewing machine, eating cake and drinking tea. And gossiping. There was loads of gossip.

'I've heard there's a big romance going on between Mairead and the flower hunter,' said Hilda.

Several ladies nodded.

'Mairead's become a dear friend on mine,' said Ethel. 'I hope they do get together and it all works out for them. She's a lovely young woman.'

'The flower hunter is away a lot,' Hilda added. 'He goes off on his yacht for months. I wonder if he'll trim his sails and settle down at his cottage.'

'From what I hear,' Ethel confided, 'he's ready for settling down.'

'I noticed the lights were on in the beemaster's cottage when I drove here tonight,' said Judith.

Ione perked up. 'The beemaster's back?'

The women laughed, causing Ione to blush.

'I was just asking,' she said, and concentrated on stuffing a fairy's wing.

I stitched around the edges of a teacup coaster I was sewing for Judith. She didn't know I was making this for her. I'd already made a sewing machine coaster for the dressmaker. The fabric prints were in my stash. I thought I would use them as quilt blocks, then decided to make little gifts for the dressmaker and Judith.

'Has anyone been looking after the beemaster's cottage while he's been away?' I asked.

Judith reduced the stitches on her knitting needles to shape the top of her tea cosy. 'Tavion's housekeeper kept an eye on it. She wouldn't be there at night. That's why I think he's back. The lights were on in all the windows.'

'Where had he been?' I said.

'London. He does a lot of business there,' Judith explained.

'He's away as often as the flower hunter.' Ione sounded disappointed.

'Maybe he'll feel like settling down one day,' Ethel suggested. 'And he's usually here for most of the summer tending his hives. That's his busiest time.'

Ione continued sewing the fairy. 'I suppose so.'

Hilda giggled. 'I hope it's a hot summer so he takes his shirt off — a lot.'

The women agreed, and various comments were made about how sexy and handsome Bredon the beemaster was.

'He's got gorgeous golden hair and eyes like liquid honey, only they're blue,' said Ione, causing a ripple of laughter throughout the bee.

One of the ladies brought through another plate of cakes and started handing them round.

'Well, he does.' Ione sounded flustered. The fairy's arms and legs dangled as she continued to stitch gold thread on to the wings.

'He's a fine looking man,' Ethel agreed.

Hilda nudged Ethel. 'With eyes like blue honey.'

Ione started to laugh. 'You lot are just winding me up.'

'This community is going to be a hive of romantic activity this summer,' said Ethel. 'Excuse the pun.'

Ione stitched a smile on the fairy's face, adding the finishing touch. 'I know I have no chance of interesting a man like the beemaster, but I'm determined to enjoy liking him until I find the man who is meant for me.'

'What about you, Tiree?' one of the ladies asked me. 'You looked very close to Tavion at the party. You could hardly have been any closer unless you'd been under his shirt.'

I was shocked then realised I liked the forthright chatter. It wasn't underhand. They said what they thought and in a way it brought things up that benefited from being talked about.

'Oh, Tiree's blushing,' said Ethel.

I could feel the warmth on my cheeks. 'I've been blushing since I moved to this bloomin' cottage,' I told them light–heartedly. 'And what about you and the postmaster, Ethel?' I turned the pointy finger in her direction.

'Yes,' said Hilda. 'I saw where his hands were.'

'That was an accident,' Ethel said, trying not to smirk. 'I slipped when we were dancing and he caught me at an awkward angle.'

There was a moment's lull and then a roar of laughter.

'Stop it,' said Ethel. 'I had my cardigan on. It probably looked as if he had a grip of my bahookie.'

Hilda stared at her and grinned. 'He had his hands on your arse, Ethel.'

'And had a fumble,' Judith added.

Ethel gasped at that comment. 'He was trying to smooth down the skirt of my dress.'

'Yeah, right,' muttered Ione.

Ethel helped herself to a slice of chocolate cake. 'Well, at least I've still got some fire in my woolly tights even though I'm as old as the hills.'

'He had a feel at those as well,' said Judith, causing another round of raucous laughter throughout the sewing bee.

'Oh look who's here.' Ethel pointed at the black cat sitting on the windowsill staring in at us.

I opened the window and Thimble jumped in.

'What are you doing here?' Judith said to him. 'He doesn't usually wander down to the harbour,' she told me. 'It was Tavion who found him the last time and brought him back up to the dressmaker. That was earlier this year and it was snowing. Mairead helped as well.'

I gave Thimble a saucer of milk, and he enjoyed all the attention lavished on him by the ladies. After exhausting himself playing with a ball of wool from Judith's knitting bag, he curled up by the fire and snoozed.

Judith drove Thimble home at the end of the sewing bee night. I'd given her the teacup coaster and the sewing machine coaster for the dressmaker. Judith loved them.

'I really enjoyed this,' Ethel said to me, giving me a hug. 'If you decide to keep this wee bee going, I'd be happy to be part of it and come along to help set the tea and clear things up after.'

'Yes, I would like to have a sewing bee,' I told her. 'We'll arrange to have another one soon. What do you think, ladies?'

Everyone was up for continuing it.

'Great,' I said.

They insisted helping me tidy everything away, and with all of them chipping in, the living room and kitchen were cleared of all traces of their sewing and knitting. Apart from some stray cake crumbs, I wouldn't have known we'd had a full night of crafting and cake.

CHAPTER SEVEN

By The Sea

The sails of the boats anchored at the little harbour looked particularly colourful the next morning when I went for a walk before breakfast. The sea sparkled, the sky was light blue, and there was a feeling of summer in the air.

Filled with energy, I broke into a run along the shore rather than a brisk walk, enjoying the warm breeze blowing through my hair. It felt as if the weather had finally turned to summer a few days before June. And with it the grey cobwebs of the past two years were blown away, making me want to smile to myself as I ran. Today was going to be a great day. I could sense it.

'I wish I had as much energy as you,' a man called to me from the esplanade.

I put my hand up to shield my eyes against the glaring sunlight. I waved to Tavion and walked towards him. 'I think summer is trying to break through.'

He agreed. 'When I cut some of the flowers this morning, there was definitely more heat in the sun. I think we're in for a fine summer.'

I walked up from the shore. 'I hear the beemaster is back.'

'He is. I spoke to him this morning. His cottage is right next to my fields.'

I hesitated, wondering how to ask for news, whether Bredon was still single or had met someone in London. I wasn't planning on being a matchmaker like Ethel or Hilda, but I did want to see if Ione had any chance to dating the man of her dreams.

'Something wrong?'

'I eh, I was wondering if Bredon was dating anyone in London, or whether he's still single and unattached.'

The hazel eyes darkened, as if I'd wounded him.

'I'm not asking for me,' I stammered, sounding awkward and as if I was lying. The more I tried to explain, the more nervous I sounded.

Tavion's handsome face looked troubled. 'I'll introduce you to him, if you want, if you're ever up at my house again.'

He said it as if I'd used him and his house for the party, and now had an interest in the beemaster.

My stomach churned and I made an excuse. 'No, it's okay. I erm, I have to hurry or I'll be late for work. The dressmaker is expecting me to arrive a bit earlier this morning.'

He nodded and smiled tightly.

And we went our separate ways.

I was mentally kicking myself. I'd changed any sense of warmth, friendship and trust from one silly question. Though if our friendship was so fragile perhaps we weren't suited after all. This was the conclusion I'd come to by the time I arrived at the dressmaker's cottage.

'You look perturbed,' the dressmaker said.

I sat down at the sewing table and began pinning the dress I'd been working on the previous day. I told her about Tavion.

'Leave him be for a little while,' she advised, and I tended to agree. The aggravation prickled my skin.

We sewed quietly and I started to feel more relaxed. Sewing had always made me happy. It was such a silly thing to do, to give it up for two years. Those two years were when I needed the uplifting sense sewing gave me. I wouldn't give it up again. Not ever.

I heard Judith working in the kitchen and the kettle going on. Oh how I wanted a cuppa.

Judith wandered through. 'Have you had breakfast? We're going to have ours. Scrambled eggs, grilled tomatoes and toast.'

The scrumptious smell wafted through. I'd skipped breakfast and driven up to the cottage. The churning feeling in my stomach had eased and now I felt hungry.

We sat at the kitchen table having breakfast. I noticed they were using the coasters I'd sewn for them.

'The dresses have arrived in Hollywood,' the dressmaker told me.

I stopped munching my toast.

'They've been approved,' she said. 'They're planning the photo shoot for the promotional poster.'

I breathed, relieved.

'They love the dresses,' said Judith.

'In fact, they love them so much they want the other two dresses.'

I paused. 'When? No, don't tell me...'

The dressmaker was nodding and her lips curved into a smile. 'Are you up for another day of pandemonium?'

I laughed and nodded.

'I'll keep the two of you fuelled up with cups of tea and cake,' said Judith.

'We're on the home straight with the sewing,' said the dressmaker. 'The vintage style dress needs the most work to finish it. Fiddly goldwork on the bodice mainly. I'll tackle that if you tackle finishing the other dress. It's ready for the top layer of silver threading. I'll pin it on if you sew it. I'll show you exactly the effect I'm looking for.'

'Okay, I'll tackle that.'

The dressmaker leaned back in her chair. 'Great.' She looked at both of us. Judith didn't notice. She was too busy scooping scrambled eggs on to a piece of toast. 'And I have a piece of news from Hollywood.' Clearly even Judith didn't know this. 'They've invited me to attend the movie premiere in London.'

I was delighted for her. 'I hope you said yes.'

'Crowds and big events aren't my thing,' the dressmaker said, 'however, I thought about it and decided — why not.'

Judith was surprised and seemed as delighted as me. 'You're going to the London premiere?'

'I wouldn't miss it,' the dressmaker told her. Then she added, 'They said they would send me two tickets.'

Judith immediately assumed the dressmaker would choose me to go with her.

The dressmaker added, 'I asked if they'd send me three tickets, so three tickets are winging their way here.'

Judith almost choked on her scrambled eggs. 'We're all going to the premiere?'

'I wouldn't go without you Judith, or Tiree.'

Judith couldn't contain her excitement and stood up. 'But it'll be on the television and in all the magazines. We might have our photos taken.'

I joined Judith and ran around the kitchen shouting, 'Yippeeeeee.'

On the surface, the dressmaker remained smiling, calm.

I stopped. 'There's something you're not telling us.'

The dressmaker shrugged. 'Well, if we're going to the premiere, you know what we're going to need.'

It dawned on me. 'Dresses.'

The dressmaker burst out laughing. 'So there could be a lot more sewing pandemonium. We've got weeks until the actual premiere. However, our dresses will have to be sensational. We are after all representing our work, as dressmakers.'

Judith flopped down on her chair. 'You're both going to have to outdo yourselves sewing dresses on a par with the Hollywood ones.'

'We don't want to outshine the stars,' the dressmaker emphasised. 'But it's tempting to raise the bar a little, isn't it, girls?'

'Oh yes indeedy,' I said.

They laughed at my response to the challenge.

'So we'd better finish this breakfast and push on with pandemonium level one,' said the dressmaker.

The three of us tucked into our breakfast, and suddenly the day had taken yet another turn for the better.

'I hope the film world is ready for us,' said Judith.

The dressmaker shook her head. 'They'll never be ready for us, Judith. Not ever.'

After breakfast, I tackled the top layer of the silver threading on the dress.

'I've pinned it on like this,' the dressmaker said, instructing me. 'Here's how to create a stunning silvery effect. Watch this.' She took the silver thread and laid it on a layer of the dress fabric. The dress was made from various tones of grey and silver chiffon. The silverwork was to enhance the styling on the skirt. 'If I put the thread here, it looks okay. If I put a metallic green thread underneath it, the silver pops and shines brighter. You won't even see the green. You'll only see the silver. It's a trick of the light.'

I blinked. 'That's such a clever way to create an amazing effect.'

'Can you finish it from here?'

'Yes.'

For the rest of the day we worked to finish the dresses. Fuelled by Judith's tea and shortbread, we had them packed and ready to be picked up for posting.

'Hollywood? You're going to Hollywood?' Ione gasped when I met her the next morning during one of my runs along the shore. Somehow the latest gossip had become muddled.

'No, it's a Hollywood movie. They're having the opening in Los Angeles, and then a premiere in London. We've been invited to the London one.'

'Oh my goodness. That's so exciting. When is it?'

'Not for weeks. We're making our own dresses. The dressmaker is designing them for us and we're sewing them ourselves.'

'You'll have to take loads of photographs and text us all about it.'

'I promise I will.'

'If the dressmaker and Judith want their hair done, remember I trained as a hairdresser, specialising in colouring. I don't want to mention to them or appear tactless, so perhaps you could drop the hint that a tint to blend in the silver in their hair would be very flattering.'

'I'll mention it.'

'I'd love to get my hands on Judith's hair. That salt and pepper doesn't do her any favours. She's got such pretty features. I could transform Judith into a golden blonde bombshell. Can you imagine?'

I couldn't at first.

'Judith is naturally light brown. I could even make her a stunning brunette. If I was her though, I'd go for the blonde.'

'I'll talk to Judith about it.'

'Do it now if you can, before they start making their dresses. Their hair colour could influence what fabrics they choose.'

I nodded. Ione had a point.

'I tried to work in hairdressing, and although I liked it, I loved the sewing more, especially making fairies. I think you have to follow doing what you love. I still do women's hair around here on the side. I keep my hand in. The colours I use are gentle, nothing harsh and I'm fussy about conditioning. I'd love to do the dressmaker's hair. I met her once a couple of years ago. I remember thinking how lovely her hair was, still plenty of blonde mixed in with the silver. She had it pinned up in a chignon, but it's long and straight. A blonde colour would blend the silver quite well. As she's a natural blonde, it would suit her skin tone.' She glanced at my hair. 'I wouldn't colour yours. It's beautiful and blonde as it is. If you

60

want, I'd trim the ends for you nearer the time, give you a blunt cut so your hair was all swishy and silky.'

'Thanks, I'll take you up on that.'

She smiled. 'Let me know what they say. I'll see you soon at the sewing bee. I'll bring hair colour swatch samples with me and my laptop with photo styles,' she said, giving me a wave and running on.

I was sure the initial excitement of the Hollywood premiere would subside and we'd get on with our work and normal routines while working on our dresses in the background. For the moment though, the news was the hottest topic.

Ethel waved me over to her cottage as I headed back to mine.

'Judith phoned me with the news,' she called to me, standing at the front door of her lovely blue cottage. It was one of the more traditional–looking cottages with flowers growing round the door. 'Have you got time for a cuppa?'

'Of course.' I went inside and looked at the spinning wheels in the living room which extended on to another room. Shelves were stacked with knitted items, scarves, shawls, jumpers and lots of yarn.

Ethel came through with tea and biscuits. We sat down beside the fire to chat.

'Judith phoned to tell me about the premiere in London, and to ask if I'll look after Thimble while you're all away for a long weekend. It sounds so exciting.'

She wanted to know the details and I told her everything including making our dresses.

'Have you told Tavion?' she asked.

'No. I haven't spoken to him.'

'The gossip will reach him by the end of the day.'

I nodded.

'So will you be continuing the sewing bee, or will you be too busy with other things?'

'I'm definitely continuing the sewing bee. My plans for that haven't changed. I'm hoping you'll come along to the next one.'

'I certainly will and I'll let the other ladies know it's still going despite all the Hollywood glam.'

'Speaking of glam, Ione has offered to do our hair. She's bringing colour swatches with her to the sewing bee.'

'Ione's enthusiasm for things could generate enough energy to power all the cottages along the coast.'

'I like Ione.'

'Me too, and she's starting to make a name for herself with her fairy dolls and home decor designs. She works hard and deserves any success that comes her way. As do you, Tiree.'

'Thank you, Ethel.'

I finished my tea and promised to chat again soon.

I told the dressmaker and Judith about Ione's offer.

'I'd love to be a blonde bombshell,' said Judith. 'When I was younger, my husband didn't want me doing anything fancy with my hair, and by the time I was on my own I'd lost the notion to colour it.' She looked at herself in the sewing room mirror. 'What do you think?' she asked the dressmaker.

'It seems like a fine idea to me.'

'Will you get yours done?' Judith asked her.

'Why not?'

And so Judith said she'd talk to Ione at the sewing bee to discuss the glamour plan as she called it.

During the following few days so many ladies asked when I was having the next sewing bee that I decided to have it on the evening of my first day off — the warmest day since I'd arrived. June brought out the beauty of the coastline. The sky was a summery blue and the sea tempted me to go for a swim. Another day, I promised myself, when I'd dug out my swimsuit or sewn one. I quite fancied making a vintage style halterneck polka dot. Turquoise and white, like the sails of a yacht that was heading out to sea.

I spent the morning exploring the area, walking along the shore, watching the boats set sail from the harbour.

On the way back I bought flour, butter, sugar and other items for baking, then went back and started making cakes and scones.

I enjoyed having a day at the cottage and did a bit of sewing. I pieced together a quilt and included some of the fabric scraps the dressmaker had given me. I machined some of it together then put it aside to reorganise my sewing room. I pushed two tables together where my sewing machine was set up to create a larger cutting table surface. I extended my sewing machine table with a second table so I could use it for cutting and sewing.

I ate lunch in the kitchen with the door open, and afterwards I pottered around the garden. One part of the garden had a flourish of blue flowers — love–in–a–mist, delphiniums, cornflowers and viper's bugloss. Lily of the Valley, one of my favourite flowers and large white daisies grew near the kitchen door. There were other flowers I wished I could identify, but I was no expert when it came to gardening. I snapped photographs with my phone, intending to ask someone, perhaps Tavion, what they were.

I hadn't seen Tavion since we'd last spoken. Maybe he was avoiding me or busy harvesting his flowers. I preferred the latter. I'd started to miss him, and he crossed my mind quite a lot considering my thoughts were filled with sewing, patterns, organising the sewing bee, baking cakes and planning what type of dress to wear to the premiere. In the quiet moments it was Tavion I thought about, his face I saw, remembering how we danced together, how it felt to have his arms around me.

The sewing bee ladies arrived in a flurry of excited chatter and again loaded with sewing projects. And knitting.

Mairead arrived with Ethel. It was now official — Mairead was dating Fintry the flower hunter and living in his cottage. As Mairead was a botanical illustrator and experienced gardener, I asked her to help me identify some of the flowers in my garden while Ethel, Hilda and other ladies took over the kitchen, making tea and serving up the cakes I'd made and the selection most of them had brought with them.

'That's Veronica blue flowers,' said Mairead. 'There are some lovely blue flowers in this garden.'

'Veronica blue. I'll remember that one,' I told her. Mairead was around the same age as me and very easy to chat to.

'Can I set up my sewing machine on your table?' Hilda called to me. 'I see you've rearranged your sewing room.'

I went back inside and helped her set it up. 'I thought this would give us more space for fabric cutting.'

Hilda had a bag of fabric squares with her. 'I thought I'd show some of the ladies how I make a quilted sewing machine cover.'

'Brilliant.' I moved my sewing basket aside so she could lay out her little quilt blocks.

'I find the five and six inch squares, especially if they're a selection of pastel printed fabrics with lots of florals, sew up beautifully into most quilt designs,' Hilda explained.

Several women had gathered round to learn the techniques.

I left them to it and went to chat to Ione who was setting up her laptop in the living room near the front window. Fading light shimmered off the sea. The evenings were becoming longer.

'I brought the hair colour swatches.' She held up a sample of them. 'Judith, come and see these colours in the light. I think this shade would be lovely on you.'

Judith put her knitting down and studied the colours. 'I do like that, Ione.'

'You'd look amazing. I could do your hair tomorrow if you want. This would let you try it well in advance of the premiere in case you don't like it.'

'That's a great idea,' said Judith. She looked at me. 'Do you think you could manage tomorrow morning with the dressmaker if I popped along to Ione's house to get my hair done.'

'Yes, of course, Judith.'

Other ladies huddled round to look at the colours. Ione opened up photo images on her laptop that allowed various hairstyles to be superimposed on different faces.

'I took photos at Tiree's party recently,' said Ione, pulling up the pictures on the screen. 'I've cropped these.' She had close–ups of Judith, me, Ethel, Hilda, the postmaster and Tavion. Ione tapped away at the keyboard and used the photograph of Judith to try various hair colours and styles on her. Some of them were outlandish, and we began laughing.

'I'm up for going blonde,' said Ethel, 'but that bouffant just isn't me.'

While trying to manipulate the images, Ione accidentally clicked on Tavion's face. A roar of laughter erupted as Tavion became a blonde bombshell.

'Oh, I'm saving that.' Ione saved a copy of the image. 'That's a keeper.'

The women encouraged her to create more mischief and we ended up laughing and giggling as Ione transformed Hilda in to a purple and orange haired punk, gave the postmaster a cockatoo quiff, and turned me into a dark haired diva.

'Have you any photographs of Bredon?' said Hilda.

'Silly question,' Ethel murmured, teasing Ione.

'Okay, so I may have quite a few snaps of Bredon,' Ione admitted. 'These were taken last summer when he was swimming down the shore.'

The women gasped.

'There's not a lot of fabric in those trunks,' one of them said, pointing to the image on the screen.

'Have you enlarged parts of that?' said Ethel.

'Nope, it's *all* him,' said Ione.

'What other men can we have a look at?' asked Hilda.

'I've got a photo of Fintry.' Ione glanced at Mairead, seeking permission to put it up.

'Let's see,' said Mairead, leaning over to take a peek.

'Fintry was down at the harbour. He's got his shirt open to the waist,' said Ione. 'Not that I was looking,' she added, smiling at Mairead.

'What would Fintry look like with dark hair?' said Mairead.

Ione changed Fintry's blond hair, covering it with a short, dark, style.

'Hmmm,' said Mairead. 'He's better with his golden blond.'

Ione gave him a wild look with long hair blowing around his shoulders.

'Can you send me a copy of that one?' said Mairead. 'I'll tell Fintry he looked really different last year before I met him. To wind him up. It'll be worth it to hear him explaining he never looked like that.'

'I'll email a copy to you,' Ione promised.

Between ogling the local men, having fun with the hairstyles, sewing and eating cake, the evening flew in. We were all rather disappoint that another sewing bee was finished.

Ione checked the time and everyone got their coats on and started to leave. 'It's only just after nine o'clock,' she said to Judith. 'Do you fancy coming back to my house? I could have your hair done before midnight.'

'Great, let's do it,' said Judith, and set off with Ione.

Ethel left with a printout of the postmaster. We'd made a joke poster that had a picture of the postmaster with wild hair. We'd added the caption: Would you lick a stamp from this man?

'I'll stick it up on the post office notice board without him seeing,' said Ethel. 'That'll teach him to fondle my bahookie.'

CHAPTER EIGHT

Vintage Glamour

Judith's hair was hidden under a silk headscarf when I arrived at the dressmaker's cottage. The morning sunlight streamed through the kitchen window, so Judith wasn't wearing it because it had been raining.

'It's fine,' said Judith, catching the toast as it popped out of the toaster. 'I wanted you both to see it at the same time.'

'Phew,' I said. 'I thought it had been a disaster.'

The dressmaker sat at the kitchen table. 'Come on then, Judith. Let's have a gander at your hair.'

Judith put the toast in the rack, stood in front of us and took the scarf off.

I don't know who gave the loudest gasp. Probably the dressmaker.

'You look stunning,' she said.

Judith gave us a twirl.

'It's beautiful, really beautiful,' I told her. And it was.

Judith sounded delighted. 'Ione styled the front a wee bit to give my hair some lift.'

'I love the colour,' I said.

Judith smiled. 'It's like champagne.'

'I'm not waiting,' said the dressmaker. 'Phone Ione and tell her she's got another client. Book me in for some glamour. Look at the shine on your hair, Judith. It's glistening. If mine comes out half as nice I'll dance around the living room.'

Judith phoned Ione. 'The dressmaker and Tiree love my hair. Now the dressmaker wants her hair done too.' She paused. 'I'll ask her.' She turned to the dressmaker. 'Would tonight suit you? Ione's up to her eyeballs sewing a batch of fairy orders. She's embroidering the wings all day, but she's offered to colour your hair this evening. She'll even come here if you want.'

The dressmaker was already nodding. 'Yes, tell Ione to drop by tonight.'

And so the appointment was made, and during breakfast we discussed what type of blonde the dressmaker would be. Champagne or chic blonde? Decisions, decisions.

We'd started work in the sewing room when the postie delivered the mail. Judith ran through waving a letter in the air. 'I think it's the premiere tickets from London.'

The tickets were being posted from the film company's London office. Their logo was emblazed on the front of the envelope.

The dressmaker opened the envelope. 'Yes, it's our tickets. This is your ticket, Tiree, and this one is for —'

A loud meow sounded from the doorway and Thimble stood there gazing at us.

'No,' the dressmaker said to him, 'this is for Judith. You're going on your holidays that weekend to stay at Ethel's cottage.'

Tail up, Thimble turned and padded off.

Included with the tickets were instructions on dress code. Evening dresses were required. A timetable of when to arrive and what to do was also included.

'I'm feeling nervous,' Judith admitted. 'We're really going, aren't we?'

'Yes,' said the dressmaker. 'And it's going to be very glamorous.'

While working on the sewing, we chatted about what types of evening dresses the three of us preferred. The dressmaker had a file of pattern designs — some ostentatious, others classic, all gorgeous.

'At least we've got several weeks to plan and sew them,' I said. Then I remembered a dress pattern I'd designed years ago. I'd never finished it. It never seemed quite right. I explained about this to the dressmaker.

'Do you still have the pattern?' she asked me.

'Yes, I saw it the other day when I was organising my sewing room. It was in a folder with other designs. I thought about adding it to the scrap book, but then I stuffed it back in with the other patterns.'

'Pop down and get it,' the dressmaker said. 'It'll be lunchtime soon. I'd like to see your design.'

While Judith made a start on cooking lunch, I drove down to the cottage and hurried through to my sewing room. I found the pattern. And that's when I noticed someone moving in my back garden. I peered out the kitchen window and blinked. Was I seeing things? What was Ethel doing crouched down, hiding behind my bramble bushes?

Then I saw the postmaster stepping over the fence at the side of my cottage and searching around the garden. I hurried out.

'Is Ethel in there?' he pointed to my cottage, while at the same time, Ethel peered over the bushes and shook her head at me.

'No, she's not,' I said to him. It wasn't a lie. Ethel wasn't in the cottage, she was hiding in the bushes. Clearly hiding from him.

I noticed the poster in his hand.

'When I catch her, I'm going to skelp her cheeky wee arse.'

'It was only a joke,' I said.

'I know. I love it.' He laughed. 'I've been wondering all morning why customers were coming in, giving me funny looks and making comments about licking my stamps.' He smiled cheerily and before leaving he said to me, 'Ethel and I used to date years ago. Do you think there's any chance she'd like to get back together with me?'

Behind his back Ethel stared at me, slightly panic stricken, and shook her head.

'Eh, no. I'm sorry. I think Ethel's happy being on her own and getting on making her yarn.'

He sighed but seemed to have expected my answer. 'Never mind. Flirting and fun is fine for now. Never say never though, eh?'

He stepped back over the fence and headed along to the post office.

'He's gone. You can come out now, Ethel.'

'Sorry for the intrusion. I'd have seen the day I could've outrun him. Your cottage was the nearest hiding place.'

'You can hide here anytime, Ethel.'

I drove Ethel to her cottage and then went back to the dressmaker's cottage for lunch.

'This pattern is exquisite.' The dressmaker admired the design while Judith made custard to pour over our treacle sponge pudding. We were celebrating apparently.

'The bodice has never been right,' I said. 'And I think I was over ambitious with the styling.'

The dressmaker shook her head. 'No, the dress just needs tweaked here and there. I like the styling. It's actually very vintage glamour. If you want, I'll play around with the design and see what I can come up with.'

'Yes, please.'

'There would be no limit to the fabrics for a dress like this, Tiree. Tulle and velvet spring to mind. Very grand. The type of dress that really makes an entrance.'

I couldn't wait to see what she came up with.

When I went home to make dinner, leaving the dressmaker and Judith to get ready for Ione, my grass had been cut and a note was pinned to the front door of the cottage. *I've been cutting the grass for this cottage for the past few years as the owner found it difficult to tend as she got older. Out of habit, and obligation, I'd promised to give the lawn its first cut this year. Promise kept. No charge. (Though tea and cake would've been nice). Tavion.*

My heart squeezed just seeing his name.

I put the note in my bag, left my bag in the cottage and went for a walk along the shore. The sun was mellow. Everything was burnished in its evening glow. The sea was calm and fragments of copper–coloured sunlight sparkled on the surface. I walked without thinking of the time or the distance, heading back along the shore grass that gave a heightened view of the sea and the entire bay.

Mairead waved to me from a distance. She was in the flower hunter's cottage garden working with Fintry. A pang of longing for that type of life with someone I loved went through me. I waved back to her and continued to walk along the shore.

I thought about Tavion. Maybe that's what it was — I'd built up feelings for him in my mind, from afar. And yet...how clearly I remembered the first time I saw him as he peered at me through the post office window. A handsome man I'd thought then, and still did. Kind by all accounts, including the dressmaker who emphasised that he'd searched for her cat in a snow storm for no other reason than it was the right thing to do.

I'd seen the photographs of the flower hunter and the beemaster on Ione's laptop. They were both handsome men, of that there was no doubt, but they didn't affect me like Tavion did. There was something about him. Perhaps the dressmaker would define it as a feeling, an atmosphere — a sense of being content just dancing with him, making dinner together, carrying my bags on that blustery day.

70

Oh yes, I'd heard the rumours of his dalliance with a woman in the city. I'd also heard he'd met up with her to agree not to see each other again. According to Ethel, whatever sporadic meet ups in the city they'd had, their relationship had run its course and ended with both wishing the other well. These things happened. It didn't taint Tavion. Not in my eyes. In fact, it helped explain where he'd found comfort outwith the local community. Everyone knew everything, or near enough, about those who lived here. I liked that aspect. It made it easier to trust Tavion. No one had a bad word to say about him. Including me.

A pink and purple twilight arched across the sea by the time I headed back to the cottage, which looked particularly pink in the evening glow.

I decided to bake a cake for Tavion that night and take it up to his house the next morning before going to work with the dressmaker.

The early morning sun made the fields near Tavion's cottage particularly lovely. The Victoria sponge cake I'd baked for him was carefully wrapped and sitting on the passenger seat of my car. I reckoned I couldn't go far wrong with a sponge cake.

I'd washed and dried my hair and let it fall around the shoulders of my cotton dress, one I'd made myself from a vintage floral fabric.

I parked in the driveway in front of Tavion's house and knocked nervously on the door.

No one was home.

He must be working in his fields I thought and drove off in search of him. It was doubtful he'd be down at the harbour shops at this early hour.

Part of a field had been harvested while the other part yielded a fair crop of flowers that looked ready for cutting. Other fields belonging to him rippled with colourful sweet peas and beyond it sat the beemaster's cottage. I thought I caught a glimpse of Tavion and headed down a narrow road towards the pretty cottage. Tall hedges prevented me from seeing whether it was Tavion, so I kept driving until the cottage was in clear view. By that time I'd attracted the attention of Bredon who was busy working in his garden.

The road came to a dead end so I couldn't drive nonchalantly by. The man I'd assumed was Tavion was someone else. A farmer by the looks of the tractor vehicle he trundled off in, heading across the nearest field.

Although I'd seen photographs of Bredon, I understood why the ladies fancied him, actually seeing him in the flesh — and I use that term in the truest sense because he was barely wearing the shirt on his back. It was white cotton, worn unbuttoned. The breeze and momentum as he strode towards me blew it open to reveal his lean torso and smooth as silk chest. His honed muscles had a honey–gold tan. I tried not to stare.

He obviously thought I'd come to visit him, for whatever reason. Maybe he was expecting a woman with blushing cheeks carrying a Victoria sponge. He smiled, glad to see me.

If I hadn't had the driver's side window open I wouldn't have had the breath knocked out of me as this gorgeous specimen of golden haired manliness leaned on the roof of the car and smiled in at me.

'Good morning.' He spotted the cake immediately. 'Is that for me?' The hopefulness in his voice made me struggle to say no.

Before I could explain that I'd mistaken a farmer for Tavion and that the cake was for him, Tavion came driving up the path, blocking me in. He got out of his car and had a look of — what's going on? He could well ask.

'Were you up at the house looking for me?' said Tavion. 'My housekeeper phoned me. You'd driven off by the time she got to the front door.'

'Yes. I wanted to thank you for cutting my grass.'

'And she's baked me a cake,' said Bredon. He glanced up at the sky. 'A beautiful woman and a beautiful day. And cake. What better start to the morning could a man ask for?'

'Indeed,' Tavion said, sounding as if the words choked him.

'No,' I said to Tavion as he marched away. 'The cake was for you.' But he didn't hear me, or didn't want to.

I recognised the crunch of the gears as he reversed back up the narrow road.

'Was it something we said?' Bredon asked, smiling at me, totally unaware of the turmoil he'd helped cause and the churning of my stomach.

'Did you spend the night with the beemaster?'

72

Judith's comment hit me as I walked into the dressmaker's cottage. Her hair was in huge sponge rollers. The dressmaker was on the phone in the living room, and so we went through to the kitchen.

'No, I didn't.' I kept my voice down.

'A farmer saw you at the beemaster's cottage very early this morning. He phoned the postmaster, who phoned Ethel, who phoned me.'

'I was looking for Tavion.' I explained what happened. 'And now Tavion thinks I baked the cake to entice and flirt with Bredon.'

I flopped down on a chair and noticed the dressmaker's sketch pad with her fashion illustrations lying on the kitchen table. 'Is that my dress design?' I turned the drawing around.

'She's been working on it. It's been sheer chaos since you left last night.'

I hardly dared ask. 'Did Ione colour her hair?'

Judith's rollers wobbled as she emphasised how gorgeous it had turned out. 'It's subtle and yet very effective. It makes her hair look like it used to. And Ione put rollers in my hair and told me to sleep with them in overnight. I kept waking up thinking I was being abducted by aliens. I'll give it a comb through after breakfast, but with all the gossip flying around this morning about you and the beemaster, I haven't even started cooking the tattie scones.'

Judith got her skillet out while I studied the dress illustration. I could see that the dressmaker had elongated the design and restyled the neckline and shoulders. I loved what she'd done to it.

'She's on the phone to the film company who want vintage dresses made for a television period drama.'

'Is she going to accept their offer?'

'Yes. It's now for four dresses, all geared for one of the characters, the leading lady. They emailed illustrations of the set designs. It looks very grand. Two dresses are for what they call 'standing scenes' and the other two are for dancing at the balls. The dresses will have to look stunning for both types of scenes. It's all quite complicated. I'm glad it's the dressmaker and you who'll have to make them.'

Judith browned the tattie scones and slid them on to a warming plate while I flicked through the illustrations.

The dressmaker finished her call and came through. Her hair was pinned up, but I could see the colour change. It lifted her features and was extremely flattering.

Judith called the order on our breakfast chit–chat priorities.

We discussed the dressmaker's hair, the vintage dress deal, Judith's delicious tattie scones hot from the skillet, and finally my supposed scandalous behaviour with the beemaster. All of this gave me a hearty appetite. Thankfully Judith had cooked extra tattie scones.

The beep of a van horn interrupted our discussions.

'It's Big Sam,' said Judith. 'He's delivering some parcels for us to the city.'

I gave Judith a hand to carry them out. One of them was a hat box, apparently containing a hat the dressmaker had made to match one of the dress orders.

Sam smiled when he saw me. 'Ooooh,' he grinned and pointed. 'I heard about you buzzing around the beemaster, Tiree. What will Tavion think, eh?'

I knew exactly what Tavion thought.

'It was all a misunderstanding,' Judith told him firmly. 'It's Tavion she's daft on. The cake was for him.'

I remembered I'd left the cake in the car and went to get it, preferring not to become inveigled in their conversation. Sam seemed to take Judith at her word. I thought I'd only cause more gossip if I said something.

'Are you still taking the cake to give to Tavion?' Sam asked. He eyed it hopefully. 'Or is it going begging?'

I handed Sam the cake. 'Enjoy.'

He put it in his van, gave us a cheery toot of the horn, and as he was reversing, he called out to Judith, 'I meant to ask you. How many radio stations can you pick up with those things in yer heid?' He laughed and drove off.

'Shite,' Judith muttered. 'I forgot I still have my rollers in.'

'Is life always like this around here?' I asked Judith as we stood for a moment outside the cottage. The trees and greenery created a deceptively calm ambiance.

'Yes, and it's not even the last week of June yet. Then you'll experience sheer chaos, mischief making and scandalous behaviour in its most concentrated form.'

74

'What happens then?' I asked her.
'The summer fete.'

I had all day to think what to do about Tavion to make things right while we pushed on with the sewing. I learned a lot from the dressmaker about dress design. Phone calls and emails were exchanged between her and the film studio. She emailed rough sketches of initial ideas and this led to them being so impressed they wanted her to design another two dresses for a secondary female character. She replied and told them we were up for the task.

It fascinated me to see how she worked. She'd made dresses for a couple of television shows before, and for a stage play. 'It's like the photo shoots for the magazines,' she explained to me. She'd done a number of those, particularly in the past few years. 'We have to take into account that simply sewing a dress, authentic in detail for the era, isn't enough. This isn't real life we're designing for. These dresses have to come across well on screen. The Hollywood dresses have to look amazing in real life for the premiere events and photograph well, but these new dresses aren't for the red carpet. They're only for on–screen dynamics. They must look like they belong when worn by the characters.' She showed me the set designs the studio had sent her, which were like illustrations in themselves. 'If we make a dress in shades of deep blue, it'll blend into the decor, and we want the main character to stand out. She's a fish out of water. She doesn't belong where she's ended up with this rich and powerful family. Although her dress is beautiful and suits the era and doesn't clash with those around her, we want her to stand out more than the others.'

'Because she doesn't belong with them?' I said.

The dressmaker nodded. 'This other character, the secondary love interest is extremely attractive, but not a temptress, and she does belong in the world she's in. So we have to make sure her dress blends more with her environment to help create a feeling of belonging.'

It was those details that perked up the studio's interest even more as the emails and calls went back and forth. Obviously, they knew her quality of dress design was excellent, but they hadn't anticipated she would take so many things to this level.

She made a toile, a mock–up, of one of the dresses using a shimmering fabric cut on the bias. She asked me to put it on and waltz around the living room to see if the skirt flowed well when I was dancing. Satisfied that it did, this was the first dress fabric and styling she chose to photograph and email to the studio.

I'd never cut many dresses on the bias, but by the time we'd finished at around six in the evening, I felt I'd had an intensive lesson and would now use the technique with confidence.

Key features were silk fabrics, bias cut, with metallic thread details. The colour tones were subtle — champagne, lustrous pearl, truffle, teal and muted tea rose. I put all the little spare scraps of fabric in my bag to add to my book collection and for quilting.

As I was leaving the dressmaker said to me, 'I hope you try again with Tavion.' Her tone had encouragement in it, though she'd said earlier she didn't want to meddle.

I smiled at her. 'I'm not giving up on Tavion just yet.'

I'd decided to ask Bredon to assure Tavion nothing intimate had gone on between us and that the whole situation was a misunderstanding. I thought about phoning Bredon, but decided to speak to him in person, just a quick visit on my way home.

The lights were on in his house. Even though the sun still had some warmth in it, the sky had deepened to a bronze and pink sunset. I wore a short sleeve top and a lemon flowery print skirt I'd made from a remnant of cotton. The skirt was a simple design with an elasticated waist. Nothing fancy, just something I'd run up in my sewing machine.

Bredon was working outside in his garden, tending his hives. He wore his bee keeping clothes and lifted the protective hood when he saw me.

I parked the car and walked past one of the hedge rows that separated the fields from his garden.

Unfortunately, I hadn't noticed a tractor going past, spraying fertiliser and I got the tail end of it up the back of my skirt. It was only a few splashes but enough to cause a stink if I sat with it in my car.

Bredon hurried me inside his cottage and through to the shower. 'Get cleaned up. I'll find something for you to wear. A shirt should do.'

Luckily, my shoes had missed being splattered, so all that was wasted was my skirt. Yes, I could wash it, but it was only a cotton print I'd made in an evening, and getting the marks out of the pale lemon fabric wouldn't be worth the hassle. I'd make another one. I didn't like the thought of the smelly doop having been on it.

I showered, dried myself with one of the clean, white fluffy towels in the shower room, and then peeked round the door. I heard Bredon come back in.

'I'll leave this shirt for you on the bed.' His bedroom had an en suite bathroom. 'Are your shoes okay?'

'Yes, not a mark on them.'

'Come through when you're ready. I'll put the kettle on. Tea or coffee?'

'Tea, thanks. Milk, no sugar.'

I fussed around, towel dried my hair and brushed it through. I put his shirt on. The soft, cream linen hung like a boho dress on me. I wore my shoes and wandered through to the living room, just as Tavion walked in carrying a box of seedlings for Bredon.

'Oh, great,' Bredon said, coming through from the kitchen with a tray of tea and biscuits. He smiled at me. 'My shirt looks like a dress on you.'

Coming out of Bredon's bedroom, wearing his skirt, hair damp obviously from having had a shower. It. Looked. Bad.

'I'll put the seedlings outside in the garden for you,' Tavion muttered to Bredon, glaring at me while he said it.

CHAPTER NINE

Strawberry Ice Cream Kisses

Sewing vintage style dresses and organising the next sewing bee kept me busy. I hadn't seen or heard from Tavion the past week. I made no attempt to give him a cake or ask Bredon to explain anything.

'Let things settle,' the dressmaker advised me.

I totally agreed.

We were having lunch in the garden, after sewing all morning with the patio doors open, letting the warm air waft through the living room and into the sewing room. Sewing velvet bodices and machining seams on other dress orders was intense work. Every aspect of the top stitching and French seams had to be perfect.

Judith set lunch up outside on the patio table. While we ate lunch — a crisp salad and roast chicken, Thimble snoozed in the sunlight on the lawn.

'Are you coming along to the sewing bee tonight?' I asked Judith.

'Yes, I'm knitting a fairy pattern. Ione's fairy dolls have given me the notion to knit one. It's my own pattern. I think I'll make the wings from some of the gold organza you used for one of the Hollywood dresses, and stitch them on to the fairy with gold thread.'

'The fairy sounds lovely, Judith,' I said.

The dressmaker's blonde hair shone in the sunlight. 'Do you still have the shirt Bredon loaned you?'

'Yes,' I said.

'Don't let Ione take it back to him for you. I've a feeling she might offer to do this. It would be an excuse for her to go to his house. She'll only end up broken hearted.'

'Okay. Do you think he'll ever be interested in Ione?'

The dressmaker looked doubtful. 'Things can always change, but I have no inkling of them being a couple.' She shrugged. 'Of course, there are so many things going on around here, and my mind is filled with all the new designs. So, for the moment, I don't see things working out for Ione with him, but that could change later in the summer.'

The phone rang. Judith answered it. It was the postmaster. She called out from the living room to the dressmaker.

'The postmaster is organising the stalls for the fete. He wants to know — do we want a stall this year?'

She shook her head. 'No, we've got far too many things to do. Tell him I will contribute to the fete fund.'

Judith relayed the message to him and then came back outside.

I helped her clear the dishes and take them through to the kitchen. We'd just put scoops of strawberry and vanilla ice cream on to three fluted plates and were about to tuck in when the doorbell rang.

Judith went through to answer it. We thought it would be a courier.

Moments later, Judith came running through to us. 'It's Tavion,' she whispered urgently. 'He wants to plant the bulbs you ordered.'

'I'd forgotten about them,' said the dressmaker. 'I ordered them months ago.'

Tavion came wandering through wearing tight–fitting jeans and an open–neck pale blue shirt with the sleeves rolled up. My stomach knotted just seeing him. He'd obviously been out in the sun and had gained a summer tan that emphasised his gorgeous hazel eyes.

He looked at me as he explained to the dressmaker about the bulbs. 'You ordered them in January. You wanted them planted in the summer for the autumn. It includes the autumn crocus. They've just arrived. It'll only take ten or fifteen minutes to plant them. They'd suit being over beside the trees.'

She could hardly turn him away, especially as he was standing there with a bag of bulbs and tools to plant them. Was it an excuse to see me? My heart thundered in my chest. I hoped so. I really did.

'That would be great, thank you, Tavion,' the dressmaker told him.

Thimble woke up, stretched and wandered over to make a nuisance of himself while Tavion planted the bulbs. Tavion didn't mind and moved the cat's tail out of the way so he could prune a couple of the rose bushes while he was there.

'We're having ice cream. Would you like some?' Judith offered.

He glanced at me before replying. 'I wouldn't mind. It's a hot day.'

Judith went away to get him ice cream, and the dressmaker picked up Thimble. 'I'll take this bundle of trouble out of your way to let you finish planting the bulbs.' She carried the cat inside, leaving us alone in the garden.

We were quiet for a moment and then, without turning round, he said, 'Are you taking part in the fete?'

'The dressmaker is too busy this year, but Ethel has asked if I'd like to share her stall. She's suggested we have a sewing bee and yarn stall. We're going to discuss it with the ladies at the bee tonight. I'd like to do it. What about you?'

'I'll have my usual flower stall.'

'Ethel says the fete is usually very busy and attracts people from all over the area.'

'It's popular.'

He finished the planting and stood up, but kept the distance between us. He smiled awkwardly and then went to go inside.

'Nothing happened between Bredon and me,' I called out to him.

He stopped and looked round at me. 'I know. He explained the situation.'

'If he explained then why do you seem so awkward with me?'

'Here's your ice cream. Strawberry and vanilla.' Judith came outside to the patio and handed him a dish, spoon and napkin. 'Sit down and enjoy it.'

He sat down opposite me at the table.

Judith sensed the atmosphere between us, shot me a look, and went back inside.

Tavion ate a mouthful of ice cream and then said, 'Judith looks different. So does the dressmaker. They've had their hair done. Was that your doing?'

'No, it was Ione.' I told him about the movie premiere in London.

'The three of you are going to a Hollywood film premiere in London?'

I was almost offended by the disbelief in his tone. 'Yes, we are. We're designing our own dresses and hoping to look glamorous.'

'You could wear anything and still look lovely.' He kept his eyes on his food as he said this. He took another mouthful of ice cream.

'Be careful. I might take your compliment seriously.'

'I hope you do.' He looked over at me. 'Though we'll probably fall out within the next ten minutes.'

The toot of a horn sounded at the front of the cottage.

Tavion continued eating his ice cream. 'Make it two minutes. That sounds like Sam's van. He's planning to ask you to go with him to the dance after the fete.'

'What?' My voice sounded like a manic squeak.

Tavion shrugged his broad shoulders. 'So I've heard.'

I got up from the table. 'What should I do?'

His reply was casual. 'Run for the hills, *tell him you're marrying me*, or accept his offer to go to the dance with him.'

'What?' Had I heard right? He'd thrown the, '*tell him you're marrying me*,' into the excuse mix so unexpectedly. 'You're kidding, right?'

'No, run. I'll tell him you got chased by a bumblebee.'

'That's not what I meant,' I hissed at him, hearing Sam's voice as Judith let him in.

Totally thrown by Tavion's remark, and not wanting to deal with Big Sam, I resorted to using Ethel's technique and made a run for it and hid behind the rose bushes.

'Where's Tiree? I thought she was out here. I was sure I heard her,' said Sam.

'She had to buzz off,' Tavion explained nonchalantly.

I peered through the rose bushes at the two of them. Sam eyed Tavion's ice cream.

'Strawberry ice cream, eh?' Sam said to him.

'And vanilla.' Tavion finished a mouthful of it.

'Some men are spoiled rotten,' Sam remarked.

'Do you want some ice cream?' Judith called out to him.

'Yes, please.' Sam sat down at the table.

Oh no. How long was I going to have to crouch behind these bushes?

'You should eat your ice cream in the kitchen,' Tavion advised him. 'It melts too quickly out here in the sun.'

Sam got up. 'I think I will. It's a scorcher of a day. What are you doing here anyway?'

'Planting bulbs over at the rose bushes. You go inside. I've still something to tend to over there.'

81

Sam went inside. From the kitchen window the dressmaker waved at me and smiled.

I was still hiding when Tavion came over. Without warning, he lifted me up, put me over his shoulder and carried me to the hedge that led on to a field.

'What are you doing?' I whispered urgently.

'Taking the alternative route out.'

Tavion carried me round the side of the cottage and then to where his car was parked out front. He put me down, opened the car door and said, 'Come on, Tiree. I'll bring you back once Sam's gone.'

I got in the car.

'I'm quite capable of telling Sam I don't want to go to the dance with him,' I said.

'I know, but some things are awkward. Tell him another time. Let's abscond for an hour, just you and me.'

I smiled at him, and he leaned across and kissed me before driving off.

'You taste of strawberries,' I told him.

'So do you.'

'Where are we going?'

'My house. There will be no one there except us. I want to talk to you without any interruptions.'

It was a short drive to Tavion's house. He parked in the driveway and we went through to the kitchen. He opened the kitchen door wide to let the breeze in. I watched him pour two tall glasses of fruit juice topped up with lemonade, ice cold from the fridge. And I felt the warmth rise in my cheeks. Seeing him again, remembering the last time I'd been here, how close we'd danced that night. I'd never forgotten it. I wondered if I ever would. Tavion was gorgeous and he affected me in all sorts of ways that made me want to feel his strong arms around me again. And to kiss him again. The kiss in the car was so unexpected. It happened and was over before I'd had a chance to savour the moment. I wanted more — kisses that lingered on the lips. Kisses to remember, always.

'Hot day,' he said, handing me my drink. It felt cold against my skin, and yet inside, I was burning. Did he know? Had he any idea how he affected me?

I nodded and smiled.

We sat outside on the garden furniture. A large turquoise umbrella shielded our table and chairs from the sun.

'I want to apologise,' he said, 'for jumping to the wrong conclusion about you. I don't know why, or perhaps I do. You make me nervous, excited, happy, wary, all at the same time.'

'Wary?'

'Yes. Wary of what will happen if I let myself fall in love with you, and then you leave and go back to your old life in the city. Wary of becoming involved. Wary of wanting to ask you to have dinner with me and where it all will lead.'

'That's a lot of wary.'

'It is. And I'm not sure how you feel about me. The cake was a good sign. After I'd had the sense to realise you'd baked it for me, and you were looking for me, I thought — maybe she likes me.'

'I do, yes.'

'Things are going to get crazy busy around here with the fete, and it's one of my busiest times, so it's not the perfect time to ask you out. However, I wondered if you'd like to have dinner with me and over the next couple of weeks, we could try not to fall out, cause misunderstandings or...'

'Take a shower in a strange man's house?'

He nodded and smiled. 'That would be a great one to add to the list.'

'I'd like to add one,' I insisted.

'What's that?'

'Kiss me.'

He leaned over, gazed at me and then kissed me, giving me the lingering kiss I'd wanted. After several moments, he pulled back and said, 'Does that get a tick box on the list?'

'Oh yes, and a gold star.'

He laughed and kissed me again, and again.

Tavion finally drove me back to the dressmaker's cottage. The curtains twitched. We'd been spotted. He kissed me anyway.

'I'll see you tomorrow. I can't cancel the sewing bee, not tonight.'

'I don't expect you to,' he said. 'Dinner tomorrow though. Dinner at my house. Around seven?'

'I'll be there.'

I watched him drive off.

The dressmaker and Judith grinned at me.

I put my hands up. 'We're taking things slowly,' I said before they had a chance to comment.

Judith nudged the dressmaker. 'Yes, we could see that.'

'Sam saw Tavion lift you up and run off with you,' said the dressmaker. 'Just so we don't get the blame for all the gossip.'

I sighed. 'Sam will tell everyone, won't he?'

They nodded.

'You'll be the talk of the sewing bee tonight,' said Judith.

'Maybe I should ask Tavion to run off with me again?' I joked.

'Don't you dare,' Judith told me. 'We've the sewing bee stall for the fete to discuss — as well as gossip.'

CHAPTER TEN

Sewing & Knitting

The sewing bee attracted even more members. As it was a lovely summer evening, I opened the kitchen door and some of the ladies sat outside on the garden furniture to stitch, knit and chatter.

'The sewing bee has become very popular,' Ethel said to me. 'You might have to end up asking Tavion if we can use his house for the occasional busy evening.'

'A lot of people have turned up because they want to be part of the sewing bee stall at the fete,' said Judith.

'At this rate, we'll need two or three stalls,' said Ethel. 'I'll ask the postmaster to allocate them if you want.'

I looked around at all the buzz — the sewing machines were occupied, patterns were being cut, Ione had brought her new fairy dolls and softies to sew, Hilda sat in the living room showing several members how to paper piece quilted picnic blankets, while Mairead tried knitting a gossamer shrug with Ethel's new sea coloured yarn. Knitters from Ethel's knitting bee were there too, sewing everything from cushion covers to soft toys. One member used my overlocker to machine the edges of a large piece of floral printed satin to make a sarong for the summer. This sparked a lot of interest and when she'd finished hemming it, several ladies tried it on and wanted to make one. Even me, and I hadn't had time to sew a swimsuit never mind a sarong to wear with it.

And all the while there were smiles, giggles and gossip about me, Tavion and Bredon.

'Do you want me to take Bredon's shirt back to him?' Ione offered.

'No, it's fine. Tavion is handing it in when he's delivering more bulbs,' I said.

'Ione, how do I stuff this fairy?' A woman held up one of Ione's fairy doll patterns and an ice lolly stick. 'Should I shove the stuffing in the legs first or the arms? Your fairies never have bumfles in them.'

Ione went to show her how to create a bumfle free fairy doll, while Ethel showed Mairead how to unfankle her yarn.

For a moment I looked around at the organised chaos. I smiled to myself and went through to the kitchen to make more tea and coffee for everyone. Hilda had brought a gallon of homemade lemonade to the bee and this was being enjoyed by the ladies outside in the garden. I wondered what some of them were up to and went out to have a look. They were papercrafting. One woman showed the others how to cut and fold a paper cottage and little sewing machine.

'I love the sewing machine.' I lifted it carefully so as not to crush it.

'They make cute wee ornaments,' the woman explained. 'I know this is a sewing bee, but I promised the ladies the last time I was here that I'd bring my papercraft patterns with me. I hope that's okay, Tiree.'

'Yes, of course.'

'I'm still going to sew a strawberry and seahorse cushion,' she added. 'Thanks for the patterns.'

'Could I have the pattern for the flowery cat?' one of them asked.

I nodded, and went in to get her a copy.

Ethel and Judith had taken charge of the tea–making.

Over tea and cake we discussed what projects the members of the sewing bee would make for the stall. We agreed to have a large stall next to Ethel. Ione and Hilda already had their stalls but still wanted to be part of the sewing bee stall. We agreed that a variety of crafts such as papercraft would be included along with the sewing.

'I'll make a quilted sewing machine cover,' said Hilda.

'I'd like to sell my new Daisy Fleabane fairy dolls and other little fairies,' Ione added.

I made a list of the items. 'This would be a great collection of things to sell at our stall. We'll have everything from rag dolls to tea cosies and cushions to quilts.'

Later in the evening Ione asked me, 'What will happen to this cottage if you marry Tavion?'

The women stopped sewing and knitting to hear my answer. 'We've only just started dating.'

'Yes, but if you like each other, maybe you'll become engaged this summer,' said Ione. 'You two might get married before Mairead and Fintry.'

Ethel spoke up. 'Yes, what if you and Tavion are the hot romance that ends in marriage this summer. The dressmaker said she felt that someone would.'

Judith agreed. 'The dressmaker sensed there would be romance.'

'What if it's another couple?' Mairead suggested. 'It's only June and the forecast is that the summer is going to stretch into September. It's going to be one of the warmest summers in years apparently.'

'We'll just have to wait and see I suppose,' said Judith.

The sewing bee finished at around nine, but the sun shone as if it was nearer seven in the evening. Long, lingering bands of gold streamed across the sky and reflected off the sea.

Hilda opened the front door of the cottage and gazed outside. 'Look at the sea. Doesn't it make you feel like going for a swim and being a wee bit adventurous.'

'What's stopping us?' said Ione. 'It's a gorgeous night.'

'Common sense, no towels and nothing but our knickers,' said Hilda.

'Common sense is overrated,' I said. 'I've got towels, and unless someone's gone commando, we're all wearing knickers.'

They gazed longingly at the sea, and at each other, and then they all speeded up.

'I'm up for it,' said Ethel, cheering everyone on.

I grabbed a pile of towels from the linen cupboard. 'Help yourselves.'

Clothes were cast aside amid a flurry of activity and wicked laughter. Blouses and T–shirts worn with their knickers were the outfits of choice. That's what I wore.

'Half decent, half scandalous,' said Judith, borrowing my shower cap, on Ione's advice, to protect her hair from the sea water.

Two women who'd turned up to the bee wearing dresses and cardigans decided to take their dresses off, wear their undies, but cover up with their cardigans.

We left our belongings in the cottage and charged down to the shore which was just across the road from the cottage. The air was warm, but Ethel warned us the sea could be a bit cold. No one cared. Screams of glee mixed with shivering gasps as the water wasn't quite as warm as the evening air.

'Once you're in the water's fine,' Ethel assured them even though she still had her woolly cardigan on to cover her essentials as she put it.

'You're only up to your thighs, Ethel,' said Ione, tip–toeing near the edge.

'I'm worried my knickers will stretch if they get soaked. I dry them flat when they come out the washing machine at home.'

'Wring the water out later,' Hilda shouted to Ethel, before diving under the surface.

Mairead joined Hilda, and so I plunged into the sea along with them. The water was mildly warm. We gasped when we came back up to the surface.

Our noisy shenanigans attracted attention.

Big Sam stopped his van on the esplanade and jumped out. 'What are you lot up to?' he called over to us.

'What does it look like?' Ethel shouted to him.

He threw his shirt and jeans off, kicked his boots to the curb and ran down on to the sand.

'Gangway,' Sam yelled and dived full force into the sea.

He emerged near me and went to lift me up, but someone else beat him to it.

'Tavion?' I gasped. 'What the...?'

Tavion held me in his arms. 'So this is what you get up to, eh? Sewing bee? Yeah, right.' And then he kissed me before throwing me into the sea and laughing. I emerged spluttering and threatening to get him back.

'Throw me, throw me,' Ione shouted excitedly to Tavion.

'If you insist,' Sam said before Tavion could reach her. She screamed as Sam threw her up in the air. The splash she made soaked Ethel's cardigan, but all Ethel did was laugh.

Sam pointed to Hilda's wet blouse. 'I can see your chookies.'

'You shouldn't be looking,' Hilda told him, unfazed by his comment. Then she gave us a nod and we piled into Sam. He was big and strong, but no match for a shoal of sewing bee ladies intent on relieving him of his boxers.

Hilda threw his underpants on to the sand.

'Come on,' said Sam. 'Give me back my pants.'

We ignored him.

I continued to swim and have fun with Tavion.

Ione sighed loudly. 'I wish Bredon was here.'

Mairead stood on the shore. She waved and called to Fintry who was working in his flower garden. She beckoned him to join us. And he did. Seeing the flower hunter in a pair of tight–fitting swimming trunks made the ladies evening extra memorable.

Mairead and Fintry swam along the coast. They were both good swimmers.

'I haven't been swimming in years,' I said to Tavion.

'We'll have to do this more often. We've a whole summer ahead of us.' He kissed me passionately. 'And hopefully a whole future together.'

I smiled up at him as the sounds of the laughter and raucous behaviour faded away, leaving me feeling there was just Tavion and me. 'I'd like to hope so.'

He pulled me close and I felt his heart beat. The warmth of his bare chest, dripping with water, pressed against me.

We stood waist deep in the water. 'I never imagined I'd meet someone like you, Tiree. From the first moment I saw you, I've thought about you every day. I'm glad the postmaster asked me to take you to the dressmaker's cottage.'

'I'm glad too.'

He leaned down and kissed me again, and again.

There were cheers from the ladies.

Sam had given up asking for someone to throw his pants to him. He grabbed the shower cap from Judith's head. 'I'll give you your hat back later, Judith.'

He used the hat to cover his predicament, though we all got a view of his backside.

'I can see your bahookie,' Ethel shouted at him, causing the other ladies to whistle and giggle.

We all fooled around in the sea for a while after Sam left. The fading sunlight glistened on the surface of the water. The night felt magical.

Then we saw flashes of light coming from the esplanade. I saw a man with a long lens camera, a young man, acting furtively.

'Awe to blazes,' muttered Ethel. 'We've been spotted by the local razzapattzi. That wee weasel will sell the photos to the papers in the city. I can imagine the headline and the slant of the story.

Summer swimmers in Scotland go for a dook with their woolly cardigans on.'

Ethel wasn't far wrong. We made the evening papers the following day. Ethel and her cardigan, as she stood in the sea, made the late edition.

'I'm rather envious of the fun you all had,' the dressmaker said to me, reading the paper.

'It was a grand night,' said Judith, making toast for our breakfast before we started working on sewing the vintage dresses.

'There's still the fete to look forward to,' I said. 'Not long now until Saturday.' The bee members had made numerous items and I'd stored them in the spare bedroom of my cottage. Judith had knitted tea cosies and she'd also made a silk sarong.

Judith poured our tea. 'I have to be honest with you, I love my sarong. I don't want to sell it. I want to keep it. Can I just contribute the money to the stall fund?'

'Yes, of course,' I said. 'In fact, I want to keep mine too.' The dressmaker had let us choose silk and satin fabrics from her collection, and they were so lovely I didn't want to sell mine either.

'Well,' said the dressmaker. 'You've sold your first two items before the fete has even started. I may even make one for myself. You've put me in the notion. It'll be cool for wearing on summery days like this in the garden, though I prefer wearing mine like a dress. And speaking of dresses, have we all settled on what we'll wear to the premiere?'

We nodded.

During any spare time we had we'd started selecting fabrics and designs for our dresses. The dressmaker had redesigned my original dress, the one I'd designed ages ago that was never quite right. I'd decided to wear it to London. She also designed a fantastic silver dress for Judith that really flattered her. We'd opted for lots of silk, satin and chiffon. The chiffon skirt of the dressmaker's gown was going to look like stars scattered across the sea. My dress had a velvet bodice and long, flowing skirt made from layers of gold tulle embellished with crystals. The premiere was several weeks away which gave us time to work on our dresses and enjoy the summer.

I'd shown Tavion my dress design and he wished he could go to London with us. We promised to take photographs and I planned to capture footage using my phone. But this was a trip for the three of us. I was glad that it was weeks away because I was enjoying my time with Tavion. We had dinner together most nights, sometimes at his house, sometimes at mine. We fitted well into each other's lives, and I knew we had a future together. Tavion was definitely the man for me.

The fete was busy. The sewing bee stall was set up next to Ethel's stall. It was a bright sunny day. All the stalls stretched along the esplanade. Bunting fluttered in the sea breeze and the aroma of sizzling burgers and sweet candy floss filled the air, along with the chatter of the people who had arrived to enjoy the day.

Tavion's stall was one of the most beautiful. It was an array of flowers. Now and then he waved over to us. He was next to Bredon's stall and somehow Ione had wangled to have her fairy stall beside the beemaster. An extraordinary amount of flirting was going on, but that was just Ione.

The dressmaker didn't attend the fete. 'I'm having a relaxing day in the garden with Thimble,' she told us.

The chocolatier didn't attend either. I'd yet to meet him.

I'd just sold a flowery cushion when Hilda came running over to us, leaving her quilt stall for a moment. Her stall had been very popular.

'Did you see who that was?' Hilda said to Judith.

Judith shook her head. 'No, is something wrong?'

Hilda leaned close and whispered anxiously. 'The rumours must be true.'

'What rumours?' I asked.

'Aurora is coming back to live in her grandfather's cottage.'

Ethel frowned. 'He's been gone for years. His cottage is leased out to holidaymakers.'

'I know,' said Hilda, 'but I heard that Aurora is moving in.'

'She's been away for what...four years?' said Judith.

Hilda nodded. 'We thought she'd never be back, but she's moved from London and is setting up a business.'

Ethel looked concerned. 'What type of business?'

Hilda kept her voice down. 'A magazine for sewing, knitting and crafting.'

'What? Here?' said Ethel.

Hilda nodded again.

'Who is Aurora?' I finally had a chance to ask.

'She's about your age,' said Ethel. 'Very sophisticated. Very attractive.'

'And nothing but trouble,' snapped Judith.

We continued to sell our items at the stalls, and during breaks, I sat over beside Tavion, sharing a delicious burger. I also shared my pink candy floss with him.

I kissed him. His sexy lips tasted sweet. 'The fete reminds me of years ago when I used to go to the shows, the funfair, every September with my mother. It was in the city, but it always felt exciting, like a magical world. I loved going on the big wheel and gazing up at the stars in the sky.'

'You still miss her, don't you?' he said softly.

I nodded and rested my head against his shoulder. 'I'll always miss her.'

He hugged me before a customer interrupted asking about the size of Tavion's hollyhocks.

I giggled and left him to it.

Later that night, the fete dance was held in a marquee set up near the stalls. Music drifted out into the evening air. I stood with Tavion outside the marquee gazing at the sea and enjoying a breath of air. We'd been dancing for over an hour. Not that I was complaining. We just needed a quick breather before heading back in to dance the night away.

Tavion stood behind me and wrapped his arms around me. He leaned down and kissed my cheek. 'You know I love you, Tiree, don't you?'

I snuggled close to him. 'And you know I love you too.'

He kissed me again.

We stood there together, content in each other's company, looking out at the beautiful coastline and the calm, glistening sea.

'I wish it could be like this forever,' I whispered.

'I promise I'll try to make you happy. We'll have a fine life together, you and me.'

'Oh there you are,' said the postmaster. 'We were wondering where you two canoodlers had sneaked off to.'

I laughed.

'Come on back in,' the postmaster beckoned. 'You've got plenty of time for canoodling. Come and see Big Sam dancing with Ione. It's not to be missed. He's spinning her around above his head.' He held the canvas flap of the marquee open. 'Come on, it's worth a laugh.'

We followed him inside, and there was Ione and Big Sam dancing in the middle of the floor while people surrounded them, clapping to the cheerful music and having a great time.

I shouted above the noise of the cheers and the music to Tavion. 'This community really knows how to have fun.'

Tavion nodded. 'There are times when things go awry, silly disagreements and trouble, but the people who live here always go back to being what makes this place special. At the heart of everything, we like to live life to the full and share it with others.' He gazed at me, kissed me and smiled. 'And I'm the happiest man here to share it with you.'

I reached up, wrapped my arms around his strong shoulders and kissed him until I took my own breath away. 'I love you, Tavion.'

'Come on, Tavion,' Sam shouted to him. 'Let's see if you can twirl Tiree.'

Without giving me a chance to refuse, Tavion lifted me up.

'No, Tavion, no,' I yelled, and then laughed, and enjoyed life to the full.

Epilogue

The Premiere in London

The flash of cameras was as dazzling as our dresses. The gold threads in the tulle of my dress glittered beautifully. The dressmaker's design comprised of the colours of the sea embellished with aquamarine sequins, and Judith's silver dress shimmered in the evening light.

Ione had refreshed the blonde colour of Judith's hair and enhanced the dressmaker's hair with another tint of pale blonde shimmer. The dressmaker wore her hair up, but there was no disguising the beauty of it. She looked radiant, as did Judith. I wore my hair down with a few strands held at the back with a vintage diamante butterfly.

On the evening of the movie premiere in London, the weather was on its best behaviour. We'd agreed to do the same. We'd been told to mingle with the celebrities and stars outside the auditorium to give the crowds and the media a chance to see us.

London had been enjoying a heatwave. The crowds, waving and cheering their favourite stars, wore summer clothing, while sharp–suited men kept an eye on security.

Barriers lined the carpeted route into the auditorium, and screens illuminated the title of the movie along with glimpses of the trailer. Celebrity guests arrived with the actors, directors and producers involved in the film. We were part of it all. Three outsiders who, for one magical evening, fitted in.

Newspaper and magazine journalists, photographers and television news crews, interviewed the stars walking past. We saw the leading ladies wearing the dresses we'd made. It was a surreal moment.

'Doesn't she look confident wearing our fairytale dress,' said the dressmaker.

I saw how the fishtail satin moved smoothly when she walked. Oh how many times I'd fussed with that hemline so it would hang right. Seeing the beading I'd sown on the bodice sparkle under the lights made me think it was worth every stitch of effort I'd put in.

The dressmaker's designs stood out in a sea of gorgeous gowns worn by the glitterati.

The leading lady stopped near us to be interviewed by a media journalist. A camera crew captured what was said. We heard every word.

'You look amazing,' the journalist told her. 'Who are you wearing this evening?'

'I'm wearing another design by the dressmaker,' the actress explained. 'I wore her at the premiere in LA. I think I love this one even more. It's hard to decide. One dress makes me feel dramatic and mysterious, like it's got a sense to it. Something magical.' She shrugged her shoulders. 'I don't know.'

I wanted to jump up and down and point to the dressmaker shouting, 'This is her.' Of course I was well behaved and didn't utter a word. But the dressmaker knew how pleased we were.

A fashion journalist stepped in to interview the leading lady, who'd gone over to sign autographs for the fans.

'Can I ask who designed your dress?' the journalist said, while the fashion magazine's photographer clicked his camera into action.

'It's by a designer in Scotland. Her label is simply — the dressmaker. It was made exclusively for the premiere.' She went on to give information about the jewellery and accessories she wore.

After thanking her, the journalist turned and saw us.

'Wow,' she gasped. 'Your gowns are gorgeous. Are you part of the movie?' She wanted to know what parts we played, excusing herself that she hadn't had time to check the credits list.

'We were commissioned to design four dresses for the premiere.' The dressmaker explained the details while the journalist asked various questions.

'Can I have your names?' the journalist said, poised to include us in whatever magazine feature she intended writing.

'I'm the dressmaker, and this is my apprentice, Tiree, who did a lot of the work that went into the cutting and construction of the dresses. And this is Judith who is part of our team.'

The actress overheard the conversation and came over to us. She smiled at the dressmaker. 'I love your gowns.'

'Thank you,' the dressmaker said as they shook hands. 'I'm so pleased they work well for you.'

The actress was then directed away to a television crew to comment on the movie.

'Everyone's starting to go inside,' I said, taking my phone from my sparkly clutch bag. 'I want to get photos of us. Stand there, so I can capture the premiere lights in the background.' The dressmaker and Judith posed while I snapped away.

An assistant going by offered to take a couple of photos of the three of us.

'Thank you, that would be great.' I handed her my phone and she took the pictures.

We thanked her again, and then hurried along to head inside the auditorium to watch the movie. As I went to click my phone off, a call came through. It was Tavion.

'We're about to go inside to watch the film,' I whispered.

'I just wanted to tell you that I love you, I miss you and I hope you have a great time.'

'Thank you, Tavion. I love you too. I'll send pictures later tonight. Everything is just like you see in the movies — glamorous, exciting.' Then I added, 'But I'm looking forward to coming home...home to you.'

End

Now that you've read the story, you can try your hand at making some of the sewing, knitting and papercraft projects mentioned in the book. You will find these on the book's accompanying website. Here is the link: http://www.de-annblack.com/sea

De-ann has been writing, sewing, knitting, quilting, gardening and creating art and designs since she was a little girl. Writing, dressmaking, knitting, quilting, embroidery, gardening, baking cakes and art and design have always been part of her world.

About the Author:

Follow De-ann on Instagram @deann.black

De-ann Black is a bestselling author, scriptwriter and former newspaper journalist. She has over 80 books published. Romance, crime thrillers, espionage novels, action adventure. And children's books (non-fiction rocket science books and children's fiction). She became an Amazon All-Star author in 2014 and 2015.

She previously worked as a full-time newspaper journalist for several years. She had her own weekly columns in the press. This included being a motoring correspondent where she got to test drive cars every week for the press for three years.

Before being asked to work for the press, De-ann worked in magazine editorial writing everything from fashion features to social news. She was the marketing editor of a glossy magazine. She is also a professional artist and illustrator. Fabric design, dressmaking, sewing, knitting and fashion are part of her work.

Additionally, De-ann has always been interested in fitness, and was a fitness and bodybuilding champion, 100 metre runner and mountaineer. As a former N.A.B.B.A. Miss Scotland, she had a weekly fitness show on the radio that ran for over three years.

De-ann trained in Shukokai karate, boxing, kickboxing, Dayan Qigong and Jiu Jitsu. She is currently based in Scotland.

Her colouring books and embroidery design books are available in paperback. These include Floral Nature Embroidery Designs and Scottish Garden Embroidery Designs.

Also by De-ann Black (Romance, Action/Thrillers & Children's books). See her Amazon Author page or website for further details about her books, screenplays, illustrations, art and fabric designs. www.De-annBlack.com

Romance books:

Sewing, Crafts & Quilting series:
1. The Sewing Bee
2. The Sewing Shop

Quilting Bee & Tea Shop series:
1. The Quilting Bee
2. The Tea Shop by the Sea

Heather Park: Regency Romance

Snow Bells Haven series:
1. Snow Bells Christmas
2. Snow Bells Wedding

Summer Sewing Bee
Christmas Cake Chateau

Cottages, Cakes & Crafts series:
1. The Flower Hunter's Cottage
2. The Sewing Bee by the Sea
3. The Beemaster's Cottage
4. The Chocolatier's Cottage
5. The Bookshop by the Seaside

Sewing, Knitting & Baking series:
1. The Tea Shop
2. The Sewing Bee & Afternoon Tea
3. The Christmas Knitting Bee
4. Champagne Chic Lemonade Money
5. The Vintage Sewing & Knitting Bee

The Tea Shop & Tearoom series:
1. The Christmas Tea Shop & Bakery
2. The Christmas Chocolatier
3. The Chocolate Cake Shop in New York at Christmas
4. The Bakery by the Seaside
5. Shed in the City

Tea Dress Shop series:
1. The Tea Dress Shop At Christmas
2. The Fairytale Tea Dress Shop In Edinburgh
3. The Vintage Tea Dress Shop In Summer

Christmas Romance series:
1. Christmas Romance in Paris.
2. Christmas Romance in Scotland.

Romance, Humour, Mischief series:
1. Oops! I'm the Paparazzi
2. Oops! I'm A Hollywood Agent
3. Oops! I'm A Secret Agent
4. Oops! I'm Up To Mischief

The Bitch-Proof Suit series:
1. The Bitch-Proof Suit
2. The Bitch-Proof Romance
3. The Bitch-Proof Bride

The Cure For Love
Dublin Girl
Why Are All The Good Guys Total Monsters?
I'm Holding Out For A Vampire Boyfriend

Action/Thriller books:
Love Him Forever
Someone Worse
Electric Shadows
The Strife Of Riley
Shadows Of Murder
Cast a Dark Shadow

Children's books:
Faeriefied
Secondhand Spooks
Poison-Wynd
Wormhole Wynd
Science Fashion
School For Aliens

Colouring books:
Flower Nature
Summer Garden
Spring Garden
Autumn Garden
Sea Dream
Festive Christmas
Christmas Garden
Christmas Theme
Flower Bee
Wild Garden
Faerie Garden Spring
Flower Hunter
Stargazer Space
Bee Garden
Scottish Garden Seasons

Embroidery Design books:
Floral Nature Embroidery Designs
Scottish Garden Embroidery Designs

Printed in Great Britain
by Amazon

81681716R00061